Wildwood

WILDWOOD
Fairy tales and fables re-imagined

by

KATE KASTEN

ISLET PRESS · IOWA CITY

By the same author

Better Days
Ten Small Beds
The Deconversion of Kit Lamb

An earlier version of "Ever and Anon" was
published in *ParaSpheres: Extending Beyond the
Spheres of Literary and Genre Fiction*, edited by
Rusty Morrison and Ken Keegan; Omnidawn
Publishing, Richmond, Calif, 2006.

TO SANDRA DE HELEN
who taught me to be whimsical

✌ Contents ✌

'EVER AND ANON

At first the Prince thought of riding headlong into the wood. He fancied the prospect of galloping through the castle doors on his noble steed and cantering straight into the Princess's chamber. There, he would lean from his charger and lift the storied beauty onto the saddle. He had always imagined her waking to his kiss charmingly bewildered to find herself atop a horse.

But the stallion was of too grand a girth to negotiate the forest's solid mass of brambles. Nor, in any case, would the Prince like to risk sacrificing his horse to the voracious appetite of the wolves rumored to guard the castle entrance. Thus, the Prince had proceeded on foot.

Now, wielding his dagger, he slashed the last of the vines and roots that obscured the great portal. It emitted a rusty groan, yielding to his staunch shoulder. He stepped inside.

Here was a majestic hall, where a hundred or more lords and ladies sat at a table before a sumptuous meal. Behind each chair, attendants hovered on the point of taking away a plate or cup, but every eye was closed, and every bosom heaved and fell in the slow movements of sleep. The room resonated with snores. Even the dogs under the table took no advantage of the unprotected feast, but lay curled and twitching in dreams of foxes and rabbits.

The Prince scanned the throng for one particular countenance. All the chairs were occupied but one. On it an embroidered cloak lay casually tossed as if its owner had stepped away for a moment. Insensible to his bruises, wounds, and aching limbs, and with no thought to the deep gashes made in his hands by the ravening wolves and piercing thorns, the Prince dashed up the grand staircase to seek the sleeping Princess.

He searched every chamber, every corner, every cubby until at last, having ascended a winding staircase to a high tower room, he found her. There she stood, not (as his old nurse had described her so often) enchanted forever in an attitude of playing a golden harp, nor (as his father's master of hounds had insisted) lying upon a bed, clad in a gown of transparent silk, her red lips parted and her limbs fallen voluptuously akimbo) but standing gracefully at an ancient spinning wheel, her dainty hand above the spindle as if she had suddenly drawn it back. A drop of ruby blood bejeweled the tip of her finger.

Luxuriant lashes fringed the Princess's closed lids and rested thick upon her cheeks, giving her the look of a sweet and innocent child. Atop the sumptuous black tresses that curled around her face and cascaded onto her shoulders was a sapphire crown. Only the faintest breath, like the whisper of a breeze, hinted that the Princess was, indeed, asleep and not transformed into a marble statue. And on her sleeping face was a touching expression of wistfulness as though some deep yearning haunted her dreams.

The Prince's ordeals—hacking his way through the fearsome, thorny labyrinth, battling the vicious wolves—were trifles compared with the reward of gazing upon her, for she was more wondrously beautiful than all the willing young ladies whom his parents had urged upon him since his coming of age. Any of those maidens could have been his for the asking: the lovely duke's daughter with the amiable trait of finding good humor in the frustrations and mishaps of life; the royal cousin in whose pleasant company he had grown up reading poetry and riding horses; the brilliant and comely Princess whose father so valued her good sense that he relied on her for advice in matters of economy and war. They stirred no ardor in him, as rumors of the sleeping beauty had already begun to exert their irresistible influence. Now, said he to himself, my obstinacy is vindicated, for never was a more radiant lady won by man.

He thought her skin as fair and unblemished as an opening petal, her figure surpassing even the imagined form which had stirred his passion as a youth and sustained him through every trial of his quest, her exquisite waist as slender as a sapling, yet joined to such bloom above as would rival the spring blossoming of a plum.

Still, he was afraid to approach her. Suppose she should become frightened on first beholding him? Might she, after a hundred years of dreaming, look upon his scratched and bleeding face and take it for a nightmare? Worse yet, what if the legendary beauty woke to his kiss and rejected his love? Suddenly he grew shy.

He stood for some while watching her in sleep. His hands bled and he held them close to his sides, though they burned to touch her. At last, longing to sweep her into his arms, he approached her with great caution and slowly bent to bring his lips against hers in a kiss so gentle, so soft, so delicate it would barely have disturbed a butterfly's wing. Instantly she awakened.

The beautiful lashes drew back over sleep-misted eyes,

and for a moment she looked, puzzled, at the face so close to hers. Then her pale complexion turned slowly rose-hued, and pinker still, as a full flush spread across her cheeks. Her dark eyes widened, her lips parted and, with exquisite tenderness she lay her fingertips on the Prince's scratched and dirt-stained jaw.

"Oh!" she said, in a breathless voice so full of longing that a mourning dove would have sounded merry by comparison. "Oh!" she said again, and at once his arms went round her, his wounded hands leaving the red prints of his bravery on her gown.

Suddenly, the palace bells began to peal and a great clamor rose from the courtyard. Lords and ladies, court musicians, serving maids and men poured forth, praising the day. There came to the two in the tower the barking of dogs, the clatter of plates, the starting up of lutes and pipes and tambourines, but the lovers heard only the drumming of their two hearts.

ᘐ

The engagement ball was given by the Prince's parents, who found much to approve in his choice of a bride. For their part, the mother and father of the Princess considered their prospective son-in-law a paragon of courage and self-command.

"You are my Prince Charming," whispered the Princess, as the two strolled among the great oaks of the palace park. The Prince took her hand and pressed it to his wounded cheek, still enflamed where the flesh had been ripped by thorns.

"I shall call you my Sleeping Beauty," he replied.

"Better your *awakened* Beauty," said she, with a sidelong smile.

Plans for the wedding proceeded anon.

It was some weeks before Charming and Beauty could tear themselves from each other's arms long enough to undertake the duties attending their engagement, but finally the lovers had to part, if only for minutes and hours. Charming, on his white steed, led the hunt to provision the wedding banquet with stags. Beauty directed the ladies-in-waiting at their embroidery hoops. Long hours of labor were required to sew the two royal crests—overlapping coronets with unicorns and leopards rampant—on all the linens of her trousseau, including her nightgowns and underskirts (which were found each morning in curious need of pressing, having gotten rumpled in another type of rampancy—so it was jested—that overlapped and crested with regularity every night).

The wedding preparations went on without cease. Two entire kingdoms were involved. Many royal relations who had made foreign alliances needed time to commission gifts and outfit ships for sea travel.

By the night of the engagement ball, Prince Charming found himself in a condition not precisely dull, so much as restive. He had drunk a goblet or two of champagne while waiting with the guests for Beauty to make her formal appearance on the grand stairway. The champagne had given him a headache. He was wondering if anyone would notice his slipping out for a canter around the Park.

At that moment he heard a common gasp of astonishment and saw the assemblage gape in the direction of the great hall. He turned, expecting to see his betrothed, resplendent on the staircase.

Instead, there stood near the foot of the stairs the most enchanting woman Prince Charming had ever laid eyes upon, excluding (he told himself without conviction) his Sleeping Beauty. Golden hair floated around the woman's face like spun silk. A diaphanous gown, made of no earthly material he could recognize, clung to her perfect breasts and reflected the candlelight in the room with the fluid shimmer of quicksilver. Her skirt billowed wide and swept the floor, yet somehow managed to suggest, as she took a step forward, the sinuous movement of voluptuous hips beneath.

Besides the perfection of her figure, her face—glorious in all details—eyes, lips, brow, chin, cheekbones—had a simple goodness, a becoming timidity; even—the Prince divined—a tremulous awe. Yes, he detected in her an unbelieving joy at being at the ball, as if—impossible to imagine!—she were not accustomed to such grand surroundings.

She had not yet seen him. To prevent her being overwhelmed —for he sensed in her an impulse to flee that might be as easily elicited as if she were a skittish gazelle—he tore off his crown and hid it behind a pillar. She drew an endearing breath of resolve, and, holding her fan against her bosom—for courage, it appeared—entered the ballroom. Oh! What rapture when the Prince saw how lightly she stepped. How gracefully, and on the daintiest of feet, so delicate that they seemed almost to be…he stared…*were*, in fact, shod in *glass*!

All other thoughts flew from his mind when he considered what grace and delicacy a woman must possess to walk in glass slippers without breaking them. The mysterious beauty, he sensed, would be a bewitching dance partner.

It is only courtesy to beg a stranger for a dance, he reasoned, stepping quickly forth. Then, great was his enchantment to find the gorgeous creature struck mute with shyness at the offer of his hand!

He led her to a protected corner. "My lady," he breathed into her ear, "be at ease. In this house you shall be accorded the reverence due a Princess. For, if royalty you are not, then royalty you should be. Your corona of golden hair alone serves better than a crown to announce your nobility."

"I...am...honored, sir," stammered the stranger and hid her face in his shoulder.

Each dance lasted a moment, yet also an eternity. The crystal slippers tinkled on the paving like droplets of rain upon a brook or bells round the neck of a lamb. The Prince's thoughts, as he felt the silken tresses brush his cheek, were bittersweet. "How shall I bear to be parted from this sylph? No, it is impossible. I must have her no matter what storm of condemnation I bring down upon myself!"

Not long after midnight, the Prince's betrothed, Sleeping Beauty, made her entrance. She was late, having caught a corner of her train on a doorstop and torn its full length just as she was descending to the ball to greet her guests. Seam-stresses had been roused from their beds to sew the train back together. When Beauty at last took her place at the top of the stairs, to the ceremonious accompaniment of French horns, the Prince was not among the throng still awaiting her appearance.

Charming entered the ballroom some minutes afterwards, too late to lead her in. In his doublet he appeared to hide something that Beauty took to be a champagne glass. She made no mention of it, nor did she pursue the subject when he apologized for his absence, claiming to have ridden out on a moonlight gallop to clear his head. There were, it was true, beads of sweat on his brow.

Beauty did not berate him, but after formally greeting the Prince's relations, politely toasting invited dignitaries, and attending to other such official duties, she left the ball, feeling hurt and aggrieved. She lay awake all night in her bedchamber, wondering, with sinking heart, if her prospective husband would prove to be a drunkard.

In the morning, one of her ladies-in-waiting, while pouring

her mistress's breakfast mead, revealed the truth: the Prince had been seen dancing for the better part of the evening on a secluded balcony with a beautiful stranger whose name no one seemed to recall.

"Forgive me," Prince Charming begged his fiancée when she confronted him. "My betrayal of you is iniquitous. No one knows it better than I." Nonetheless, he announced his determination to discover his mysterious dancing partner's identity and ask for her hand in marriage, for he felt that he could not live without her. Sleeping Beauty, desolate and rumored to be with child, returned with her parents to their realm, leaving Charming free to roam the kingdom in search of his true love.

လ

It was a scandal throughout the two kingdoms. The Prince had broken his engagement and was now traveling the land on his white steed, searching village, town, city, castle, even cottage and hut for the mysterious, shy beauty with whom he had danced.

He castigated himself ceaselessly for allowing her to elude him and was tormented by the image of that moment when, at the stroke of midnight, just as he was drowning in the blue pools of her eyes, she had suddenly wrenched herself from his arms and fled the palace, running as gracefully as she had danced, and so lightly that even in her haste to descend the stone stairs, her glass slippers did not shatter, though one was cast off in the escape. He had scooped the slipper up as he rushed after her, almost dropping it when he stumbled in the road over a pumpkin fallen off a peasant's cart. Jumping to his feet, he stared helplessly in every direction. But the beautiful stranger had disappeared into the night as if she had never existed.

ᴖ

In rain and snow, under blistering sun and glacial moon, he rode the lanes and high roads hither and yon. He ate and slept little. Everywhere he went, he carried the glass slipper and asked each woman of the kingdom to try it on. There could be only one, he believed, with foot so dainty that it could fit into the tiny, fragile shoe and also dance in it. He would not rest until he found her.

A year passed, during which he searched in vain. Finally, having sought his love in every corner of the land, he returned, haggard and weary, to his parents' home. With bowed head and broken heart, he rode up the cobbled streets leading to the palace.

Suddenly, a torrent of rain fell upon him, soaking him to the skin. Looking up in surprise, he saw that it was not rainfall, but a bucketful of wash water poured on him from a house above the street.

A young woman at the window looked out in great distress at the misfortune she had caused. Before he could get a look at her, she cried an apology and vanished from the window. Prince Charming recognized the voice at once. He leaped from his horse and forcefully entered the house, a dwelling he had visited the year before at the commencement of his search.

Three women were knitting by the fireside—a sour-faced mother and her two daughters. They stared at the intruder, astonished.

"Where is the maid who poured water on the Prince?" he demanded.

The women threw down their knitting and rushed to greet him, the mother begging his forgiveness for her careless servant. The daughters then scurried off to fetch food and drink, and cloths to dry him. But the Prince would have none of it.

He bounded up the stairs and searched the house over until, throwing open the door to a small scullery, he found a beautiful young woman dressed in rags and cowering in a corner. Instantly, he threw himself at her feet.

"Ah!" he said, gazing up at her heavenly face. "Even in rags you are the angel of my dreams."

Cinderella (for that was her name, she confessed to him later) blushed and turned away.

The Prince grasped her lovely hand. "Why did you not reveal yourself when I first came to this house?"

"Oh, Prince Charming," she replied, tears threatening to spill over her golden lashes, "how could I, after I learned who you were and that you were betrothed to another?"

"My darling," said the Prince, hanging his head, "You are a good and true creature, and I am not worthy to kiss your precious foot." But kiss it he did, and repeatedly, before fitting the glass slipper on it. Then he cried bitter tears and at last convinced Cinderella that his engagement had been broken off for a year, that Sleeping Beauty was reconciled to it, that she had already married her father's cousin—an elderly earl of considerable distinction—and now had a handsome baby boy. This defense—to Prince Charming's credit—was true.

Eventually Cinderella gave way to the hidden passion she had harbored for him all that twelvemonth, and finally, after much fear on the Prince's part that he might, still, at the last minute, lose her, they were married.

☙

On their wedding trip, Prince Charming and his bride passed through many lands. Cinderella had never seen the world, and it pleased her husband to show it to her. He directed their coachman to stop at quaint cottages, venerable churches and towns of antiquity. She admired nature in all its forms and begged to alight at each brook, bower, or hillock with a rustic view. She was entranced by all she saw.

But after awhile this idle rambling began to wear on the Prince. He found himself suffering not precisely from irritation so much as indifference. In consideration of her feelings, he did his best to hide his lassitude, but each time Cinderella urged them down yet another dusty, out-of-the-way lane, the Prince grew increasingly restless to return home to horse and hounds.

On one stifling afternoon, at the bottom of a meandering lane in the middle of nowhere, Cinderella bade the coachman stop the horses at the site of an ancient, crumbling tower.

An unusual spectacle had attracted her attention. An old hunchbacked crone was climbing from the tower window by way of a length of auburn rope. Prince Charming yawned at the curious scene. After the crone reached the ground and hobbled down the road, the Prince heard the old woman croak over her shoulder in a menacing voice, "No one shall ever have you but I!" and he looked back to see a ravishing young woman in the tower window. She displayed a look of both deep resignation and profound sadness. The Prince suddenly realized that the auburn rope was the woman's magnificent hair, plaited in a braid so thick and long it reached all the way to the ground.

Cinderella was remarking on the agile old woman's brisk progress up the lane and did not notice the younger woman at the window, but as the carriage re-traced its journey to the high road, Prince Charming made a mental note of the exact route back.

BLUNDERBUSS

Baby Bear stood by his bed and stared at the creature asleep upon it. What odd forelegs it had—long and thin—with four digits at the end of each leg, curled like fern fronds around a fifth. Its coat did not lie close to its skin like his own, but loose in folds of green and red and yellow. Edging closer, the little bear put out a paw to feel of the strange stuff, but drew it back quickly when the creature stirred. Suddenly, it opened its eyes, shrieked at the sight of him, and in an instant was off the bed and out the open window.

Mama Bear and Papa Bear rushed into the room when they heard the shriek, but they were too late to see the intruder. "It was sleeping in my bed!" cried Baby Bear, trembling with excitement. "Then it leaped up and jumped out of the window and ran into the woods!"

"What did it look like?" Mama Bear asked, wringing her paws.

"How big was it?" said Papa Bear.

"It was my size," Baby Bear exclaimed, "and it had light hair that flew out behind its head when it ran. It did not have fur, but skin that fluttered, and its face was the color of a clam. It ran on two legs like twigs, and it stared at me with round eyes as blue as robins' eggs!"

Papa Bear said to Mama Bear, "This is a goblin, there is no mistaking it. What else could account for such an appearance? You know that they can take whatever form they like."

"A goblin, yes!" agreed Mama Bear and shuddered. Papa Bear began to pace from room to room in his great lumbering way, a worried frown furrowing his wide brow. He passed through the room where the goblin had slept in his and Mama Bear's beds, rumpling the bedclothes and leaving the imprint of its head on the plump pillows. Then he strode into the kitchen. Here, three porridge bowls—one empty—sat upon the oaken table. Two chairs were drawn back from it and a third—Baby Bear's little one—lay on its side, one leg askew.

"But," said Mama Bear, following after him with Baby Bear trotting close behind, "the creature has only eaten a little porridge and broken a chair and slept in our beds. Perhaps it meant no harm."

"Goblins always mean harm!" replied Papa Bear. "They are heartless creatures with no remorse. Now that the villain has been inside our house, it will surely return, perhaps with a band of other goblins, and murder us in our beds!"

Baby Bear listened to his parents' talk and his little heart thumped.

"Hush, Papa," said Mama Bear. "Don't frighten the child!" But Papa Bear could not hold his tongue.

"Henceforth, we must lock our doors and windows when we go out and also at night when we sleep," he said.

"Yes, yes," said Mama Bear, patting her child. "That will keep us safe."

"But," continued Papa Bear, "suppose the scoundrel attempts to invade our house by force in the night?"

"Oh no!" cried Mama Bear. "What would we do?"

Papa Bear sat down then, taking Baby Bear's little chair into his paws to start to mend it. Soothed by this occupation, he considered more calmly a course of action. Presently an idea came to him. "There is a farmer at the edge of the woods," he said. "Let us go to him and see if he will give us a weapon in trade. I have heard that farmers have such things. They are long straight objects which can kill from a distance." Baby Bear's small eyes widened at this notion.

"Might not the farmer kill *us* with such a weapon?" said Mama Bear doubtfully.

"He has the reputation of being a kind man and not one to kill without cause."

"Then that is the thing we must do," agreed Mama Bear, relieved. And she ruffled the fur on top of Baby Bear's head.

"Now," ruminated Papa Bear, "what can we trade for such a weapon?"

"We can dig out the great honeycomb high up in the hollow of the old oak and give the farmer that," said Mama Bear.

"That is a good idea," said Papa Bear.

So the next day, Mama Bear, Papa Bear, and Baby Bear went to the middle of the forest to fetch the honeycomb. Soon they came to a venerable old oak, within whose vast trunk abided the rings of three centuries. Papa Bear began to climb it, but when he reached the high branches his weight was too great and the branches bent and threatened to snap. Then Mama Bear climbed up, and because she was lighter, the branches held, but her paws were not small enough to reach around the honeycomb and pull it out without breaking it.

Baby Bear begged his parents to let him try, and at last, with many cautions, they consented. He scrambled easily up the tree, and though the ground was very far below and the branches swayed and the bees flew around his eyes, he did not flinch. His little paws were just the right size to fit perfectly into the hole. Proudly, he pulled out the honeycomb and brought it down between his teeth.

That afternoon, Papa and Mama Bear set out for the farmer's house. "Keep all the doors and windows locked," they warned Baby Bear. "Do not open the door to anyone."

"Please, can't I go with you?" cried Baby Bear, for he was afraid to stay at home alone.

"No, my boy," said Papa Bear, "We do not know this farmer and must approach him cautiously. It will be better for you not to come."

"We will only be a little while," Mama Bear reassured him. "If you stay inside, you will be safe." So Baby Bear stayed home and waited.

When Mama Bear and Papa Bear drew near the farmer's house, the farmer was at his well, drawing a bucket of water. The bears waited at the edge of the forest until, looking up from under the brim of his wide straw hat, he noticed them and beckoned them to approach. "Please rest and have a drink," said he and bade his little daughter to fetch bowls from the house, which she did, casting furtive, fearful looks over her shoulder at her father's guests.

When she returned, she set the bowls on a stump, but would not hand them to the bears nor look the bears in the eye. "Don't mind my daughter," said the farmer, caressing her cheek. "Goldilocks is shy with strangers."

Mama Bear exclaimed, "What a sweet and pretty thing she is!" At this the farmer smiled broadly and stroked the child's fair hair, for the little girl was his pride and joy.

"You need not be afraid of bears," he told his daughter, trying to get her to raise her face so his visitors could see her bright blue eyes. "Bears are gentle creatures and do not eat children, as a wolf might." Mama Bear and Papa Bear chuckled at the idea of a bear eating a child. "We gather nuts and berries in the woods," said they to the farmer's daughter, "and sometimes catch fish in the stream as you do." But the little girl only bowed her head lower and would not say a word.

Then, when the farmer saw, by the bears' demeanor, that they had come to do business, he sent his daughter into the house to help her mother.

Papa Bear came to the point. "Have you a weapon that you would give in trade? We are troubled by goblins and want a means to protect ourselves."

The farmer commiserated. "Goblins are dreadful, soulless villains, it is true. I am grateful that they do not bother me, but prefer the cover of the forest." He thought for a moment, lifting his straw hat and mopping his brow with a kerchief to give him time to consider. As it happened he did have an old blunderbuss to trade, for he had been a soldier once. He had no use for the weapon now, as he owned a fine longbow, carved of the best yew. With this weapon he could easily kill the foxes who raided his hen house. He could boast, with satisfaction, that he never failed to hit his target, even at a range of two hundred yards.

"Well," said he, replacing his hat, "I have a blunderbuss I might be persuaded to give up. What have you to offer me in trade?"

The bears brought out the honeycomb, glistening and dripping with its sweet load of honey. "Why, that is the finest, largest honeycomb I have ever seen!" the farmer exclaimed. "It would sweeten our porridge for the greater part of a year without the pain of a single bee sting for fetching it!" And so he agreed to the trade. But first, because he was an honest man and did not want to cheat the bears, he cautioned them.

"A blunderbuss hits its mark only at close quarters," he said.

"But wouldn't it serve to frighten a goblin from coming into our yard?" said Papa Bear.

"Or trying to enter our house?" said Mama Bear.

"Yes, undoubtedly. But also consider," the farmer said, "that a blunderbuss is an awkward weapon and hard to load and shoot. Even men have some difficulty doing it, but a bear— though your arms are certainly strong enough—would find it difficult indeed." He paused, thinking that he had spoken rudely, and added, "Only because of the size and shape of your paws, of course."

Papa Bear asked if he might try. So the farmer went into the house and came back with the blunderbuss along with a box of powder and a pouch full of shot. He showed Papa Bear how to hold the gun and cock it and pull the trigger. Papa Bear, having big strong arms, could sit on his haunches and hold the heavy blunderbuss up to his shoulder with no difficulty, but it took many tries before he could cock the gun with one of his great curved claws and hook another into the trigger.

Then Mama Bear sat on her haunches and tried, too, for she might have to kill a goblin if Papa Bear were not at home. Her arms were not as strong as Papa's, and she could not hold the gun so steadily against her shoulder, but she could cock the gun and pull the trigger more easily than he, for her paws were smaller and more deft.

Then the farmer taught the bears how to load the blunder- buss. He showed them how to put priming powder into the pan, then pour a measured amount down the barrel and push in the shot with the ramrod. Finally, he showed them how to cock the trigger. It was delicate work, but with persistence they learned to follow his instructions. Each fired the gun once and felt the terrible jolt against the shoulder and the ringing in the ears from the thunderous noise and watched the dust rise and settle where the shot fell upon the ground. They both hoped they would never have occasion to use the fearsome thing.

At last, the farmer wrapped the blunderbuss in burlap and gave it, along with the powder and shot, to the bears. He took the honeycomb from them, and the three parted, well satisfied with the exchange.

ꝏ

When the bears returned home, they stood outside the door and called to their child. "Let us in, Baby Bear! It is your Mama and Papa." Hearing their familiar voices, Baby Bear dragged the wooden bar from off the door. When he saw their parcels, he inquired, eagerly, "Where is the weapon?" but his parents did not want him to see it.

"It is a blunderbuss," they told him. "You must never touch it. It is dangerous."

"What is a blunderbuss?" asked Baby Bear excitedly, for it sounded like something very big and interesting. But his parents were too preoccupied to answer.

Papa Bear went and hid the blunderbuss away in its burlap wrapping high atop the tallest shelf in their bedroom, where Baby Bear could not possibly reach with his little arms. Baby Bear was disappointed. He sulked all afternoon and would not eat his porridge, but his parents remained firm and finally sent him to bed.

That night, Baby Bear peered through a knothole in the door as Papa Bear brought the blunderbuss down from the high shelf and took off the burlap. He watched Mama Bear and Papa Bear load the gun and cock it and pretend to pull the trigger. He watched them practice many times, for the gun was still difficult for them to use. "*I* could do it *easily*," he whispered, imagining himself sitting very tall on his haunches, the gleaming iron and wood device propped against his own shoulder. In his imagination his shoulder was very broad indeed.

༃

After breakfast the next day, Baby Bear held his stomach and drooped his head, and Mama Bear gave him peppermint tea and told him to stay home while she and Papa Bear went to gather food. Baby Bear promised to keep the door barred and to open it only when he heard their voices and saw them through the window.

As soon as they had gone, he grasped the back of his father's big chair and pushed and pushed and pulled and pulled until he had brought the chair through the door to his parents' bedroom and placed it below the shelf. He clambered onto the seat of his father's chair and stood as tall as possible, stretching his little arms as far above his head as he could, but they were too short and the blunderbuss was out of reach.

So he climbed down and ran to the kitchen, where he took hold of his mother's chair, which was lighter than his father's, and soon he had pushed it into the bedroom, and with all the strength in his little arms, pulled Mama Bear's chair on top of Papa Bear's and stood upon it and reached and reached again, but his arms were still too short.

He climbed down once more and ran to get his own little chair, which was so small he could pick it up and carry it. For the third time, he climbed onto his Papa's chair, then pulled his own chair after him and pulled it onto Mama's. Then he stepped up onto it as easily as if he climbed a set of stairs, and now the height was just right. He reached up and lifted the blunderbuss from its place, nearly dropping it, for it weighed almost as much as Baby Bear did himself. With a mighty effort, he climbed down, staggered with it to his own bedroom, and laid it on his little bed. Then he returned to his parents' room, climbed back up to the shelf, and brought down the powder and the shot.

With a thrill of excitement, Baby Bear quickly unwrapped the blunderbuss. It was a wonderfully strange and complicated thing. He passed his paw along the smooth wooden stock and around each convolution of the brass cocking apparatus. He touched the cool iron of the trigger and the muzzle. He opened the box of powder, drew the strings of the pouch, and took out a pawful of the shot. Holding it to his nose, he breathed in its peculiar leaden aroma. Then, remembering everything he had seen Mama and Papa Bear do, he loaded the blunderbuss and cocked it.

At that moment he heard a strange sound, very faint, from outside the house. He ran to his bedroom window and looked out. There, far off in the distance at the edge of the forest, was the goblin who had slept in his bed! The goblin stood with bent back under a walnut tree and appeared to be gathering nuts, though it was too far away for Baby Bear to see clearly through the trees. The goblin was singing, not with twitters and warbles as birds sing, but in a goblin voice, full of high drawn-out tones that ran eerily up and down like the wailing wind. Baby Bear's heart raced with fear and excitement. Now, he thought, I can kill the goblin and it will never bother us again and Mama and Papa will be proud of me.

When Baby Bear tried to carry the blunderbuss to the window, it dragged upon the floor. He leant it against the wall and opened up the casement. Through the open window, the goblin's shrill tune fell louder on his ears. He struggled to hoist the blunderbuss to the windowsill. The gun wobbled and teetered in his arms. Finally he rested the muzzle on the sill and balanced the stock against his shoulder, clinging to it with one paw. Far in the distance, the goblin did not see him, but sang on and continued to gather walnuts. Baby Bear tried to keep his arm from shaking as he fit his little claw into the iron trigger. Then he took a deep breath and pulled.

The flash singed his fur, the jolt knocked him backward, and the deafening explosion rang in his ears. With a crash, the blunderbuss fell to the floor. For a moment Baby Bear was too stunned to move. Then he shook himself, scrambled to his feet and looked out the window. A small cloud of dust had risen and was settling on the ground in the yard outside the house. In the distance, the goblin stood straight, and was shading its eyes against the bright sun to peer in Baby Bear's direction. Suddenly, it scampered away and disappeared into a field of grain at the edge of the wood.

Baby Bear was breathless from having the wind knocked out of him, and he stood at the window for some minutes recovering. "Well," he said to himself after awhile, "I did not shoot far enough, but I have frightened the goblin away so that it will never come back."

But then, doubts began to assail him. In his dreams the night before, the terrible creature had chased him through the forest, its strange coat fluttering uncannily and its twig-like claws reaching out. Baby Bear had wakened just as the goblin had caught up with him and shrieked that it would tear out his eyes.

Now he thought, "What if the goblin has gone to tell the other goblins, and they return in a band to kill me!"

His arms trembling, he dragged the blunderbuss back to his bed, hauled it up, and with as much haste as his small and breathless body allowed, re-loaded and staggered with the weapon to the window again. For some while he stood balancing the blunderbuss on the sill, searching the forest for signs of goblins returning, but he saw nothing.

At last he began to relax and breathe more calmly and considered lowering the heavy blunderbuss to the floor. But all at once another creature appeared under the walnut tree. Its skin was pale, too, but it was twice the height of the first goblin. On its head was a flopping object of straw, which shaded its eyes, so that, at such a distance Baby Bear could not make out if the eyes were the color of robins' eggs. This creature was so much taller than the other—as tall as Baby Bear's father when he stood on his hind legs—that it certainly must be the leader of all the goblins.

In one hand, the tall creature carried two strange objects: stripped branches, one bowed, the other straight and held crosswise to it. The goblin shaded its eyes and appeared to stare in the direction of the cottage where Baby Bear stood at the open window clutching the blunderbuss. "At least," thought he, "I have a weapon and the creature has none." Then the goblin came striding swiftly toward the house. Though shaking in every limb, Baby Bear tightened his grip on the gun and curled a claw around the trigger. He braced himself for the flash and jolt that was sure to knock him over.

He waited for the goblin to come closer, but the creature stopped just outside the clearing and raised the crossed branches in the air. Baby Bear could make out an angry, threatening scowl on the goblin's face, and the little bear's courage almost failed him. His breath came short. His strength seemed to leave his body. Only with great effort did he manage to tilt the wobbling blunderbuss a little skyward, thinking the shot might thereby travel farther.

Then he pulled the trigger. There came the same burning

flash and stunning jolt and deafening noise in his ears, and he was tumbled backward and knocked breathless to the floor once again. But as soon as he could gather his wits about him, he rose to his feet and hastened to the window to learn the effect of his action.

A cloud of dust was settling to the ground, yards short of the tall goblin, who stood beyond it unharmed. The creature's face had lost its threatening scowl and was now fastened coldly and calmly on the face of Baby Bear, who stared back from the casement window. Squinting against the sun, the creature slowly raised the crossed branches to shoulder height and extended the bowed branch to the full length of its arm.

Baby Bear longed to run and hide under the bed, but kept his place at the window, for "While I can still see the creature," he thought, desperately, "I shall know what it intends to do." In terror and fascination, the little bear watched the goblin strike a curious posture: its lower body turned sideways toward the woods, its face and arms pointing directly toward the cottage.

Now it drew back the straight branch, and Baby Bear saw, faintly, a thread attached from one end of the bowed branch to the other, and this, too, had been drawn back, and held taut next to the goblin's cheek. Suddenly, as if by magic, the branch flew out of the goblin's hand. It flew faster than an owl can swoop upon its prey. So straight and swift did it streak through the air that Baby Bear had time only to utter one brief cry of surprise.

꒳

When Mama and Papa Bear returned home carrying sprigs laden with raspberries for their evening porridge, their calls for Baby Bear to unbar the door went unheeded, and they had to squeeze through the open casement window. "Has our child fallen fast asleep at such an hour?" they exclaimed, trying to quell their alarm over the unlatched window and the child lying in a heap upon the floor. But there was no rising and falling of the little chest in slumber, nor any yawns or sighs when they tried to nudge him tenderly awake with their great muzzles. Imagine how inconsolable was their grief when, turning him, they found the shaft, for the path of the arrow had been sure—neither too short, too high, too low, or too wide of the mark. The goblin's aim had been just right.

TWO BEASTS

Two months after she left the Beast, Beauty had a terrible dream. In it she saw her poor Beast alone and dying. His tongue lolled, and the bristles at the corners of his mouth were frothed with foam. The end of his snout was dry, his fur matted and oily. He squealed and grunted in agony.

Beauty woke sobbing and went immediately to find the ring the Beast had given her, by which she could magically return to his castle. "Oh my darling Beast!" she exclaimed, pressing the ring to her heart. "Do not die! I must lay eyes upon you again!" And on uttering these words she found herself standing in his rose garden, the Beast prostrate at her feet among the thorns.

She fell to her knees, clasped his great boar's head to her bosom and kissed the once pointed ears that drooped now like autumn leaves. She kissed his hoary snout and cloven hoofs and rheumy, weeping eyes and begged him not to die. "For I love you," she said. "Please live, so we can be each other's boon companions again, even as wife and husband." On the instant, a golden light suffused the garden. A spring breeze passed over their faces and Beauty found she was holding in her arms the splendid and radiant figure of a handsome young prince. "My sweet Beauty," he murmured. Then, folding her in his arms, he gave himself up to the desire he had harbored for so long.

༄

The enchantment was broken and the Prince restored to his former glory. For his sake Beauty rejoiced that he had cast off the guise of Beast, but for her own it mattered little. She cared nothing for his outward appearance; his pleasurable company and sympathetic kindness were all.

And so the Prince and his Beauty were married soon after, in pomp and ceremony, their love celebrated across the land at festivals, and in ballads sung by troubadours.

Never before had a prince and princess been so well suited to each other. Their long months of intimate acquaintance-ship as beast and maiden had allowed them to form the true bond of friendship and mutual compatibility so necessary for a happy marriage. In the Beast's castle they had read aloud and listened to sweet music together; they had enjoyed long walks in the gardens and often—having fallen deep in conversation—lost all track of time. Such opportunities were afforded few royal couples, who customarily wed as strangers following mercenary family arrangements. But Beauty and her Prince, as they exchanged their vows, saw reflected in each other's eyes the depths of a passionate devotion.

Even after their marriage, the Prince with his bride discovered still sweeter strains of harmony such as he could never have imagined when he lived under the sorcerer's curse.

The day he was turned to a beast, he had been hunting, and killed a boar. No sooner had he knelt to inspect his quarry than a strange man dressed in a long cloak and holding a staff appeared before him and claimed the animal as his own.

"You have shot my handsome boar, which I nurtured from birth and treasure beyond all my possessions," accused the outraged stranger. Then and there he raised the staff and cast the spell on the Prince, who felt his breeches and waistcoat split down the back. He looked hastily into a rain puddle and saw reflected there the hideous visage of a grizzled old pig with flea-bitten ears, small squinting eyes, and curved, yellowed tusks rising at each side of a considerable snout. The sorcerer had also given him a ragged tail, scaly two-toed hooves, and a coat of drab brown bristles tipped with gray. From that moment to the day, years hence, when Beauty grew to care for him, he had lived in wretched solitude and despair.

But Beauty's love had cast off this terrible curse, and the Prince could not quite believe his good fortune. "I now possess the love of the most beautiful and companionable wife any man could hope for!" he told her, and was often heard to laugh and say to others, "If the evil sorcerer but knew what a great favor he did me in spite of himself, he would be chagrined!"

This same sorcerer, passing through the Prince's lands on some malicious errand or other, chanced to hear someone quote this remark. The sorcerer was vexed to think that the Prince had benefited rather than suffered for his crime, and so it was that, one day, the evil magician appeared in the royal bedchamber, where Beauty sat alone. She was surprised to see the stranger, but graciously put down the little volume of poems she was reading and bade him be seated and tell her his business.

"My business," said the sorcerer, "is this." He drew his staff from inside his cloak, flourished it over her head and transformed her then and there into a sleek, wild sow. Upon feeling her body suddenly swell and seeing the cloven hooves emerging from her lace-clad wrists, she sprang from her chair with a grunt of horror and rushed to the looking glass. What she saw caused her to fall into a faint.

The magician waited patiently for her to revive. When after several minutes she came around, she wept and lamented her condition. "Oh, heaven help me!" she cried, "I am a beast, a beast!" But she choked back any further outpouring of emotion upon hearing the coarse grunts and squeals that misshaped her words.

The sorcerer chided her blandly. "Of what do you complain, dear Princess? I have made of you a fine sow with a well arched back and thick, russet coat, much handsomer than the one I gave your husband as a beast. You are as beautiful a sow as you were a woman." The magician walked around Beauty as if to admire her from different angles. He nodded with satisfaction.

"Please appreciate that in consideration of your good character I give you advantages I gave not to your husband. Him, I changed to a grizzled boar in what some might deem the unsightly decrepitude of age, though I personally do not take that view." Absently, he fondled his long white beard. "On you I bestow the prime of youth. I've given you sharp pearly tusks for rooting in the earth, elegant ungulate toes of a durable, horny consistency, and a tidy double row of teats, six to a side, with which you may suckle the full complement of each season's offspring. Considering the great love you and your husband enjoy for each other, I anticipate that the numbers of your offspring will be of Biblical proportions."

When she raised her hoofs in an imploring gesture, he waved back at her an admonishing finger. "Pray do not thank me, dear Princess. It is the least I can do." He frowned. "Yet I detect uncertainty upon your countenance. Can you doubt the steadfastness of your husband's affection in this event?

Consider that I made of him a hideous wreck of an animal and still you grew to love him in that guise. Do you suppose that he will stop loving you in this one of yours?"

Then he paced the room as if deep in thought while Beauty lay, half insensible, at the foot of the looking glass. At length, the magician stopped his ruminations and favored her with a disingenuous smile. "In consideration of your renowned goodness," he said, "I promise you that as soon as your husband kisses you without repugnance—nay, with the genuine ardor of romantic love—your human form will be restored to you. Thus, I predict that your sojourn as a sow will be unfortunately brief." He drew himself up with self-satisfaction. "So you see, dear Princess, I do you and the Prince a great favor." And with that, he vanished.

Alone in the room, Beauty stared at herself in the mirror. Gone was the slender waist, the delicate shoulders. Now the shapeless swelling of porcine flesh was bursting her gown at the seams. Her crown of glossy auburn hair was replaced by coarse, red bristles which covered her whole body, all but the two nostrils of her upturned snout and the cloven horns of her feet.

She tore off the scraps of her gown with teeth and hoofs and nosed frantically among her folded silks until she found a voluminous dressing gown, which, with some difficulty, she wrapped herself in, then sat down on her haunches and waited with great trepidation for her husband to return.

ॐ

"What mischief is this!" shouted the Prince when he entered the chamber and found a beast clothed in his wife's gown. "Here then!" He put his head out into the hallway. "What vixenish maids have presumed to bring a pig into the royal chamber for jest?!" But Beauty stepped forward quickly. "Husband!" cried she. "It is I!" As her voice was not her own, but a mixture of crude grunts and shrill squeals, he did not at first realize she had spoken words. "It is I," she said again, "your wife" and then weakly, "your Beauty" and collapsed upon the bed, weeping piteously as only a pig can weep.

The Prince stood in the doorway, reeling with shock. As the footsteps of the servants he had summoned came clattering down the hall, he slid into the room and quickly shut and locked the door. For some moments he could only stare at the swinish figure weeping on the bed. Then he found voice to ask what had precipitated this disaster. She winced to hear him call it this, though she considered it so herself, then told him of the magician's visit.

"Did he not grant some proviso," her husband asked, "by which he might lift his dreadful spell?" Beauty told him of the terms the sorcerer had laid down.

With only the slightest hesitation, the Prince crossed decisively to the bed, rolled Beauty over and, closing his eyes as lovers do in passion, placed a resounding kiss on her snout, then quickly released her and stood with arms unconsciously folded across his chest. Beauty did not need to look down at herself to know that the embrace had occasioned no change. She groaned and lowered her head in sorrow.

"Beauty," coaxed the Prince, with some tenderness, "Pray have patience. Do you not remember your first shock at my appearance and the weeks that passed before you were able to look at the Beast's facade and let the man beneath into the deepest part of your woman's heart?"

"Yes, dear husband," said Beauty, but she recalled that her reluctance had come before, not after, she knew him well.

He would, he vowed, grow used to her appearance and find affection for it in less time than it had taken her. But just now, he said, it would be wise to keep her circumstance a secret. "Why secret?" asked she. "When all the kingdom learned of your former predicament, they were in sympathy. Surely they will extend the same sentiment to me?"

"But that was after the fact," said the Prince, avoiding her eyes, "And then, too, I fear it would be difficult to explain to them, for if they hear of the sorcerer's condition for lifting the spell, all will know that I have failed to satisfy it—not that I won't, in time! On the other hand if we don't mention the sorcerer's condition, all the world will consider me forever cursed—"

"Cursed? You?"

"That is…" The Prince found himself at a loss for words. "…By cursed I don't mean, of course…" He became abruptly irritable, exclaiming that surely she should know what he meant to say and not condemn him for using imprecise words. Then, in a conciliatory tone, he said, "Just as you did, I must have time to recover from my natural discomposure." She nodded, averting her face, too ashamed to display her whiskered snout to him again. In a hearty tone, he said, "Allow me to go now and make my excuse to the serving maids whom I summoned. Perhaps you should stay here for the time being behind our chamber door. I'll tell them you are ill and not to be disturbed." And with that he backed away, blowing kisses that seemed to Beauty to fall dead in the air. Then he opened the door a crack and slipped through it.

Left alone, Beauty was tormented by her husband's inadvertent use of the word 'cursed'. She rose and resolutely faced the looking glass to confirm what he had beheld. In it, she saw a reflection not so different from the one that must have become familiar to him in his own mirror during the years of his enchantment.

She sank again upon her bed and remained there listless until the Prince returned a full two hours later, bearing in his own hands a tray of her favorite dishes. He would not take food himself, he declared, but would serve her, to remind her of his devotion. They sat together at a little table, where he raised the fork to her mouth.

"Well do I remember the shame," said he, "of taking meals with my nose in a plate as if at a trough. You shall never suffer such humiliation." And Beauty partook of her meal from his hands with gratitude, though she did notice that each time her snout and lips closed over the food, her husband seemed to look slightly away.

She ate but little, not only from having an appetite depressed by anxiety, but because—though she could not bring herself to confess it—the cooked meat, risen bread and baked custard did not please her. Grubs and fallen fruit were what her palate now craved.

During the first day of confinement to her chamber, Beauty occupied the time by doing what little she could to make herself presentable. She combed and curried her undercoat, cleaned her tusks with vinegar and polished her hooves with beeswax. Her husband came and went bearing trays of food but otherwise seemed unusually busy with affairs of state, which—he regretted—did not allow postponement, much as he longed to keep her company.

The Prince stayed away the entire evening. It was not until midnight that she heard the key in the door. No maid servant had come to light a candle, nor had Beauty found the will to try to do it herself. The room was dark. After closing the door behind him, the Prince made his way to the bed. "My precious dear," he said, effusively, "please forgive me for seeming indifferent to your distress these many hours. You must know that I love you more than life itself and have only been struck stupid with the pain of your suffering."

Joyfully, Beauty took a breath to reply, but the Prince hushed her with these words, "No, my darling. Do not speak. What you say to defend me will only increase my remorse. Allow me to embrace you now with all my heart, for you are dear to me in whatever form fate has chosen for you." Stumbling a little in the dark, he found the bed and swept her into his arms. She eagerly raised her face for a kiss, and kiss her he did, full and forcefully on the mouth, so that she could not but smell the heavy reek of wine on his lips. "There," he said, drawing back as if waiting, and for a moment there was silence between them and then she felt with distress the fur rise on her back.

He reached for her hand. Finding a hoof, he let it go quickly, then fumbled to take it up again, saying, "These hours of concern for you have so exhausted me, dear Beauty, that I fear my want of ardor may be mistaken for a failure of affection. Pray let us sleep so that I may wake refreshed and then do justice to your beautiful spirit." He turned and lay on the bed with his back to her. She repressed the squeals of pain that gathered in her throat, well imagining how he would receive such sounds. After hours of fitful sleep and wretched dreams, she woke at daybreak to find herself alone.

It was then she made up her mind to end her confinement and put herself at the mercy of the kingdom. Gathering courage, she stepped into the corridor and called her maids, who came running at the sound of the strange, guttural voice issuing from their mistress's doorway. They stopped in wonder at the sight of her. With difficulty, she made them understand she was indeed the Prince's Beauty, whom they had known and loved. Respecting her husband's wishes, however, she did not reveal the sorcerer's terms for lifting the spell. Afterward, the servants went about their tasks in awed silence, speaking together only when they had left the room, and then in hushed voices.

Word of the dreadful turn of events spread quickly through the kingdom. There were immediate expressions of shocked sympathy for the royal couple, as the Prince was well-liked and his bride widely praised for her kind heart.

Attired in specially made slippers and gowns altered to fit her new dimensions, Beauty now appeared in public, taking her meals as before with her Prince and his entourage in the great hall and performing the duties of princess as best she could, receiving the wives of ambassadors, arranging for state dinners, hearing and conveying petitions of the Prince's dependents. As time went on, however, Beauty could not help but notice arising among the populace certain waggish quips and jests at her and the Prince's expense. She could not fail to overhear the ribald comments regarding their predicament. Nor, she knew, was the Prince oblivious to these, for several times in his company she saw him flinch at remarks that neither of them was meant to hear.

Beauty caught snatches of her maids' conversations. "Such a vigorous and handsome man!" they whispered, "And think of the continuation of his line! Twelve squealing, stripe-backed little sons to fight for succession to the throne!" And sounds of muffled laughter ensued, with futile attempts to hush them. Beauty could see that such jibes stung the Prince and made him avoid her more.

The husbands of homely noblewomen married for their money now felt greater satisfaction with their wives, and these wives benefited by comparison to the Princess. She overheard a venerable duke advise the Prince, "You cannot be expected to put aside your natural repugnance in such a case."

It wounded Beauty to see how her husband gave his accustomed affection to his favorite hunting dogs, allowing them to lap his face and obliging them when they rolled onto their backs to invite their hairy bellies to be stroked. Even the Prince's horse he kissed upon the nose and embraced around the neck. But she, he avoided and was loath to touch.

Behind her back, Beauty was made such an object of derision and fun at court that she withdrew more and more to her rooms rather than endure the looks, glances, and titters behind fans. Did no one pity her, she wondered, as she had once pitied the Prince, nor see the tragedy in her circumstances? Who would comfort her and assure her of their loyalty? Even to her own blood relations she seemed to have become an embarrassment. Only the beggars who loitered outside the palace seemed indifferent to the alteration in her. Her generosity and responsiveness to suffering were still among her prominent traits, in spite of everything.

No longer did Beauty and the Prince read aloud together or discuss the world's news or peruse the exotic flora that grew in the royal gardens. If he engaged in such pleasurable pastimes, he did so without her. Though he ordered that all her needs be attended to, he denied her the thing she needed most—the pleasure of his company. It seemed he had to travel abroad much more often than before. And when at home, he complained of fatigue and gave the necessity of his rising early as reason for sleeping in a separate bedchamber.

Then there came the day when Beauty overheard a noble-woman confide her admiration for a certain part of the Prince's person which he could not have displayed to the woman but in a state of undress. Of all the torment Beauty had suffered until then, none was so painful as this. Heartsore and alone, she trotted up and down the length of her chamber. At last she made up her mind to confront the Prince. She called a servant and had her husband summoned to her room.

"Did you not tell me once that you loved me with your whole heart?" she demanded when he arrived. He bowed his head and was silent. "Hypocrite!" she cried. "What part of me was it that you thought you loved?"

"Why *all* of you, of course. But consider, my darling—" he seemed to choke on the endearment "—that a man needs—"

"Nay! Do not finish! I cannot bear to hear you say it. Leave me and do as you please, for I no longer care." Slowly he turned and slunk out, but the farther his footsteps receded from her door the more sprightly they sounded.

Beauty's words rang in her own ears, and she wept profusely to hear their echo, for she realized their truth. Her heart, never hardened to anyone in all her young life, was now hardened against her husband, and she cursed the day that, with a maiden's innocent love, she had released him from the magician's spell. She cursed the day her father plucked the Beast's rose and the day she herself had asked for that modest gift. Better to have selfishly requested diamonds or gold!

Then she cried out bitterly, "Oh, how I wish that my husband might live alone and unloved again as a beast, and understand truly what it is to have a broken heart!" At these words, the sorcerer appeared in her chamber once more, all smiles and graciousness.

"My dear Princess," said he. "My dear Beauty! Well, well. I see something is amiss and events did not transpire as I predicted. You are yet a beast?" Shaking his head with disbelief he pondered, "I cannot understand it. You would be the prize of any strapping boar who caught your scent. A pity your husband is a beast no longer, or at least not a more discriminating man. How could our Prince have once been intimate with your unblemished soul, yet fail to love you now?"

"Oh, sorcerer!" Beauty cried. "Have you come to release me from this spell?"

"Alas," he said with a manufactured sigh, "it is impossible, for the condition of your release has not been met." He smiled. "But your *other* wish, the one you made just now, *that* I can fulfill with pleasure."

"What wish did I make?"

"To change your husband to a beast again. Nothing could be easier if you wish it."

Beauty stared at him. Then she stood for some minutes as if in a reverie. At last she replied.

"I do wish it," she said.

"Then it is done—even as we stand talking." But a look of pity crossed Beauty's face, and the magician noticed it. Remembering her reputation for compassion, he said, "I detect a wavering. Do you wish the spell to be ameliorated in some manner? Shall we hinge it, for example, on a maiden's kiss of true love?"

Beauty thought long and hard. As she paced the floor, the sharp tap of her hooves echoed off the marble. The sorcerer waited patiently, amusing himself by observing the depth of anguish that could be conveyed by expressive grunts.

At last Beauty heaved a deep sigh and gave her answer. "No," said she. "Do not depend this spell upon a maiden's willing kiss. Never in all the world," she said, and her eyes grew hard, "do I wish to see another of my sex relinquish her heart to a pig."

THE PAID PIPERS

Wind-scattered where the mountain sealed,
odds and ends of children's things—a doll, a wagon wheel,
a shoe cast off in haste of running—tell the little ones'
delight, the Pipers' cunning. And now all day and night
the church bell rings. Yet no attendant comfort brings
the sacred knelling. No quelling of the parents'
rage and tears nor of their whispered fears:
"What new and poisonous tune may reach our ears?"

Impressive in be-robed and prosperous fat, Hamlin's
Councilors and Mayor pledge swift revenge
upon the doers of the act. "In your children's
names—" vows the Mayor, ("Ah," sighs a mother,
fondling a locket) "—and that their deaths be not in vain—"
("Huzzah!" comes the roar. For minutes, none can stop it.)
"—We'll seek the villains everywhere!" Then walks
Lord Mayor to the sacred site and mounts a banner
on its height, kisses every tear-stained face, and to
each grief-bowed shoulder gives a firm embrace.

Lord Mayor's Councilors burn a months' supply of candles
in a week, so little do they sleep, plotting how to find, and kill,
the Pipers and their ilk. Criers cry, broadsheets drip with

ink, and townsfolk gather in the streets to find out
what their neighbors think.
Now and then the villains' tune is rumored to be heard anew.
A piping like the tinkling of a bell has lured a
housewife down a well. A single note, as of a nesting swift,
has sent a shepherd hurtling off a cliff. A trilling, like
a plaintive wren's, tempts a magistrate into the fens
wherein he drowns. Such stories terrify the town, and Hamliners
demand to know why yet the Pipers are not found.

Few remember whence the murderers had come—
a rugged, mountainous land, where bands
of sorcerers against a pestilence of rats waged war
and how the Mayor of Hamlin had in secret sent
these sorcerers stores of flutes, with hope that they'd
enchant the pipes and with them rout the brutes.
For if the cunning rodents gained the upper hand,
Hamlin feared an infestation in *their* land, and so by
ill-considered plan, lavished upon crafty, merciless men
instruments of death as to a trusted friend.

Now, the secret past unknown, some in Hamlin glance,
and look askance, at neighbors known to be musicians,
if their clothing, like the Pipers', too, is pied—
mottled in spots of yellow and red—
though they, as well, mourn children, dead.
As fear holds sway, tales of treachery abound
and innocents are locked away
in secret dungeons underground.

As to the whereabouts of the Pipers and their suspected minions
there are alike no two opinions.

Lord Mayor and his Council travel far and wide—even to those
regions where most citizens' clothes are pied—cautioning
their governors in language stern and blunt: "Put other cares
aside and join our hunt, for we alone must not be left to bear
the brunt of making all the world safe. And when the
governors at this proposal chafe, Hamlin's Mayor tenders
both a bribe and threat: "Remember, all of you are presently
in Hamlin's debt. Fail us to your eternal woe, since he
who is not with us is our foe." One by one, the governors
agree, albeit most uneasily. For among their humbler populace,
no love for Hamlin Town is lost as Hamlin's soldiers
search each town and rural hut, slashing beds and
stabbing hay and burning barns where might the Pipers stay,
and those suspected take away.

A growing number everywhere begin to swear
allegiance to the Pipers. "Who better," they cry, "to rid us of
these vipers – these faithless governors and Hamlin's avenging
men? 'Tis certainly from them that all our problems stem.
Are they not as foul an infestation as scurrying mice? Do not
their depredations corrupt like crawling lice? It is the Pipers'
trade to do away with vermin, so let us now determine to
lure them from their hiding place, to fight our foes
and give them chase."

Many hold back, recalling what they've heard
of Hamlin's young, in mountain stone interred, and
of their pitiful refuse—ribbons, toys, and shoes.
They wonder, "What may happen if this perilous path we
choose?"

Despite their qualms the call goes out from lowest vale
to highest peak that certain folk the Pipers'
tuneful service seek. Thence, carried in a falcon's beak
from deep within a mountain cave,
a message is relayed: "We play our tunes
to slaughter pests, and gladly honor your request
to drive out your abhorrent guests, and in return your
oath to hate whomever we despise, and sacrifice
—if so required—your very lives, with courage.
For that, we'll liberate you from the Hamlin scourge."

So the pact is made, the promise won, and no sooner is it done
than shrieking strains as from a devil's flute do each and every ear
pollute with sounds profane 'cross mountain, ridge and hill,
and fill with horrible cacophony the air that once was still.
'Twas like the sound of

cats yowling, curs growling,
buzzards screeching, hares beseeching,
serpents hissing, rats frisking,
bats fluttering, roaches scuttling,
locusts mating, ants invading,
mice squealing, thunder pealing,
wolves wailing, hail hailing,
moles tunneling, cyclones funneling,
rain pouring, floods roaring.

A tune, in short, to set a mortal person trembling in fear,
but yet a stirring battle hymn upon a goblin's ear.

The hearing of this disconcordant tune arouses goblins
by the thousands, drawn like moths to gibbous moon.
Goblin masses, in abeyance to their masters' song,
leap upon the backs of asses, harnessed frogs,

and maddened dogs. Roads fill up with every mode
of goblinish conveyance, hastening them along.
Sneering goblins, jeering goblins, lecherous and
leering goblins, goblins savage as hyenas, goblins bestial
and fiendish. Goblins of every brand and stripe
follow the tune of the sorcerers' pipes. A bearded knave
in yellow and red is glimpsed cavorting far ahead.
Now, as one, the goblin hordes, yearning towards the alluring
sound, race madly on to Hamlin town. In a trice, they've come
to Hamlin's gate, impossible to penetrate, for sentries, sounding
an alarm, have caused it to be closed and barred. Yet –
wondrous to relate! –the gates do part by no one's hand,
and through the gap, like rats, ten thousand goblins swarm.
And when at last the swaggering stragglers past sentry boxes
strut, the city portals with a final clang swing shut.

Oh, brash country youth, take heed, and dare not climb old Hamlin's
walls to peer down on the littered square, the darkened halls.
Nor, with curious gaze seek alleys drear, where huddled Hamliners,
in dread, await such goblinish whims as make them envious of the dead.
Nay, avoid this town where hangs a pall that's poisoned
the sky for a hundred years and bids the winds refuse to ease
or the lowering clouds to clear. For to this day, without
surcease, never knowing a moment's peace, Hamliners—
governors, commoners, all—to the Pipers' tune in thrall
have lived, ever wishing, if they could, to turn back time and
bear in mind that the lesser evil is never good.

WILDWOOD

Faint from hunger, the children wandered in circles through the forest. At night they shivered with fear and cold while wolves howled around them. They huddled together remembering the oven's glowing mouth, the cramped cage, and the witch's terrible screams echoing through the trees as they ran away on legs weak with terror. They prayed to their angel mother in heaven, who had been good and kind and had tucked them into bed warmly and kissed them good-night. In the mornings, they woke curled together for comfort.

After many days of desperate searching, Hansel and Gretel at last discovered the way back to their old home, where they learned that their hateful stepmother had died in their absence. Their father shed tears of joy to see them. The woodcutter's fortunes had improved in the months the children had been gone, and there was once more enough food on the table.

Now Hansel's and Gretel's bellies were full, but their hearts were heavy with recollection and foreboding. When their father asked Gretel to bake a pan of gingerbread, her stomach turned and her fingers dropped the pan before it reached the oven. When he sent Hansel to the edge of the wood for kindling, the boy came back sooner than expected and out of breath, carrying only a few twigs.

The children woke with nightmares. Sometimes it was the witch's roaring oven that plagued their dreams, and her loathsome cackle as she vowed to pick the flesh from their bones. Sometimes it was the low, insinuating voice of their stepmother cajoling their father until in weakness he relented: "You are right, my wife. The children will be better off fending for themselves in the woods than starving with us here at home." Their father's mild visage appeared ominous in these nightmares, his eyes cold as if his thoughts were elsewhere as his children pleaded to be allowed to stay.

In some dreams they pursued a gentle, perpetually vanishing phantom into a dark place where they could not follow. In others, a house came down in flames around them. Their nighttime cries often woke their father, who began to find it onerous to care for his children alone.

ꝰ

In the neighborhood was a prosperous farmer's widow, a comely and capable woman with six healthy children. The woodcutter wooed her, and she agreed to become his wife.

He told Hansel and Gretel, "She will make a good mother to you."

"How sweet you are," said the widow to the children at their first meeting. "You shall call me Mother and have the companionship of my own dear ones." She patted Hansel's and Gretel's heads and put sweets in their pockets. But the brother and sister could not help shrinking from her attentions, remembering similar promises of kindness that their stepmother had made before she and their father were wed.

"Come, come, children," their father chided. "Do not greet the lady with closed faces. How ungrateful you appear after she has kindly agreed to be my wife and raise you as her own."

The widow's four eldest children were older than Hansel and Gretel, while the two youngest were but infants—twins of only a year. She urged the eldest forward to kiss their brother- and sister-to-be, and when her children refused, she clucked at them indulgently. "Tut tut, my bashful dears," she said.

Before his wedding, the woodcutter took the widow and her oldest four into town to buy provisions for the celebration.

"We will bring you back rich cloth and ribbons for the wedding," the widow told Hansel and Gretel. "Look after my babes while we are gone. They are too young to come with us."

She gazed fondly at her plump and rose-cheeked infants as she placed them in the children's arms before leaving. "Take good care of them, my dears," she said, "for they are my youngest, and I always have a special fondness for the youngest of my brood." And turning toward the door she added, "Mind the loaves I have set out so that you and your dear father will have bread for your supper. By the time they have risen we will have returned, but if something should delay us, put the loaves in the oven. Be careful not to burn yourselves, children. It is very hot!"

Hansel and Gretel lay the babes on the hearthrug and watched them squirm and crawl about and pat their dimpled hands together and utter squeals of happiness. Then brother and sister sat dully by the oven on its old stone tiles. Billows of smoke rose up the chimney. The children could smell its strong pine scent through the cracks in the bricks.

"Our father's wife will never care for us," said Gretel, "with six of her own and these youngest ones so sweet."

"Yes. We are not hers. Furthermore, the older ones resent us."

"How can our father have married one woman who hated children and now propose to marry another who has already six of her own?" said Gretel.

Brother and sister remembered their former stepmother's handsome face and figure and their father's pleasure when he had made up his mind to marry her, though she was known in the village to have a sharp tongue and selfish ways. Now Hansel and Gretel shared the same thought—before long this new mother would find them as burdensome as had the other and persuade their father to send them back to the wildwood.

As they listened to the cooings and gurglings of the pretty little babes, Hansel's and Gretel's hearts filled with dread. They thought of the weeks of abandonment in the forest, the stealthy footpads of unseen animals at night that made them shake with fear of wolves and witches and goblins, and the terrible hunger that made the house of sweets appear as a gift from God. They remembered the moment the witch's kindly, coaxing voice turned to a triumphant croak as she slammed the cage door shut. And the little song she sang absently to herself each time she passed the cramped enclosure:

> Crisp, crackling
> broiled children.
> Stewed, fattened,
> boiled children.
> Basted, juicy,
> roasted children.
> Tasty, sizzled,
> toasted children.

They shivered at these memories.

And now, in Hansel's mind a wicked idea formed.

"Suppose *we* were the youngest," he said to Gretel, "and we were very obedient and good. Then would our father's wife not dote on us as well, and would we not then be safe?"

"I wish it were so, but it cannot be, for these dear babes here are her youngest."

"Suppose," said Hansel, not daring to look his sister in the eye, "the babes were lost in the wildwood. Then would we not come to replace them in their mothers' heart?"

Gretel looked sidelong at her brother. "Hansel," she said, "you cannot mean that we should take them to the woods and leave them there?"

The two sat in hushed silence, contemplating the terrible thing. All the while, the sweet babies at their feet prated and squealed.

Then Gretel said, "Our father would search the wildwood over for them and soon they would be found. Then he would certainly send us away for having failed in our charge to look after them."

Hansel said, "But suppose we swear that goblins came to steal the babes and that we fought mightily to save them…"

"Fought mightily…" Gretel said, slowly, "but to no avail."

"We could cut our arms with father's axe…" Here he picked up the little axe kept in the house for chopping kindling—"and show them our wounds."

"Yes," said Gretel. "And mix some of our spilled blood with a paste made from the bluebells that grow by the door." She added, urgently, "Everyone knows that goblins' blood flows blue."

Then she saw that one of the babes had crawled near the oven. Hurrying over in alarm, she picked the baby up and laid him gently back upon the rug.

"Still," reflected her brother, "the people might go to the wildwood to rescue the twin babes from the goblins, and they would be found and we would yet not be the youngest."

"Unless," said Gretel, placing a foot softly against the other child's plump belly, for he was rolling toward the hot oven as well, "unless they were not to be found in the wildwood."

The brother and sister looked at each other frankly.

"How could that be?" said Hansel, taking his sister's trembling hands.

"If they were not in this world at all," she said, the tears rising in her eyes. They both stared at the oven and felt its heat.

Then their voices dropped to a whisper and they clung to each other and spoke hastily and in fright.

"As soon as nothing remained but ashes, we could cut our arms—" said Gretel.

"—and run to the neighbors and say what happened," her brother continued.

"That the goblins—"

"—took the babes—"

"—after a mighty fight."

"Yes."

"And when the neighbors follow us to our home, we will show them the goblin blood on the axe to prove our struggle."

Quickly, the two prepared to carry out their plan.

Then one of the babes began to whimper, and Gretel took her up into her arms to comfort her. "Oh, Hansel," she said, "I could not bear to hear them scream."

"Nor I," said Hansel. He cast his eyes desperately around the room and, fixing again on the little axe, picked it up. "We must first strike each of them a quick blow before putting them into the flames. Then they will not feel the pain of burning."

"Yes," said Gretel, "and open the oven door beforehand so that as soon as the babes are struck, we can put them in and slam shut the door without having to look at their little dead faces."

"That is the best way," said Hansel.

Tears flowed freely down their cheeks.

The room was very warm now. Hansel and Gretel heard the crackling and popping of the flames and the tiny squeals of hot air working its way through the wood. They stood and stared at the infants for some minutes as if in a trance.

Then Gretel noticed the risen loaves of bread ready on their wooden pallet. "We must do it now," she said in a quavering voice, "for it will soon be time for the others to return."

They prepared the bluebell paste in a bowl on the table and swung open the oven door. The flames sucked air with a fearsome noise. Hansel gripped the axe. To Gretel, he said, "See that the babes do not move."

Gretel, weeping, knelt down and turned the wiggling infants gently onto their stomachs. Stroking their backs, she spoke soothing words to them. "Hush, little ones," she said, then grasped an ankle of each child so it could not roll away.

Hansel raised the blunt edge of the axe and aimed it at the head of the first, at the tender place where soft brown hair curled around the cowlick. He stood poised, listening to the merry, chuckling sounds that bubbled from the babies' rosebud lips.

"Oh, how can we do this terrible deed," cried Gretel, "when the innocent little ones have done us no harm?" Hansel, still gripping its handle tightly, lowered the axe.

"We must," he said. "Think of the wildwood." And the two remembered all that they had endured there and what else might be in store for them, should they be exiled there again.

"I cannot watch their little heads being struck!" said Gretel, and she closed her eyes, as did her brother, after he had once more raised the axe and taken aim.

"Oh, this is too hard," thought Hansel, and even as he stood with axe held high to do the dreadful deed, he knew he would not be able to let it fall, and that he and his sister had no choice but to suffer a new abandonment to the wildwood.

"I can't," he whispered. "Yes," he heard his sister say, "it is impossible."

At that moment there came a violently shouted oath. The children's eyes flew open and they beheld the tall figure of their father in the doorway carrying two bolts of velvet cloth in his arms. The woodcutter threw down the cloth, crossed the room swiftly, and tore the axe from Hansel's hands. With one strong arm he snatched both babes from the floor.

"What is this abomination I have interrupted?!" he cried in a terrible, choking voice. Hansel and Gretel cowered backward and clung to each other, weeping. "Have I spawned two children so envious," their father shouted, "that they do the devil's work?! Are you monsters, that you should try to murder innocent babes?" He placed the infants, howling now, upon the bed, then strode to where the children huddled by the hearth, grabbed them by their arms and pulled them upright.

He, who had never struck them, rained blows upon their heads and shouted into their faces. "Are you fiends?" he exclaimed. "So pitiless that you would deprive their mother of her most precious dear ones, breaking her heart? See how this devoted woman has chosen for you this handsome cloth so you can dress in fine apparel on her wedding day! Would you thus throw her affection in her face?" Here he picked up the two bolts of velvet and hurled them into the oven. The flames rose to consume them.

Then he shook the children fiercely and cried, "What does your mother in heaven think to see her children turn out so!

She, who was the gentlest creature in this world. Now she cries in horror! Looking down upon this scene, she is no more in heaven but in hell! She is sorry you ever returned from the wildwood!"

Choking with sobs, Gretel pressed her hands to her ears and pleaded in a thin, strangled voice, "No, Father, please! Do not say so!" But the woodcutter wrenched her hands from her ears and shouted again, "Your mother would not forgive you in a thousand years for this sinful deed."

Hansel could not bear the anguish of his sister. The heat of the oven flushed his face. His head swam. The babes on the bed howled and the fire in the oven seemed to crackle and snap in accompaniment to his father's fury.

"Do not be so harsh to my poor sister!" he begged and laid a hand on his father's arm.

"You!" His father whirled upon his son, grabbing him by the shirt. "Unnatural boy, to lead your 'poor sister' to such an abomination! You are most to blame. *You* have corrupted her when it was your duty to protect her, the younger. You are evil beyond redemption!" And he struck his son again, as Hansel cringed and fell back.

"No!" cried Gretel. "Pray, do not hurt him!" and with all the strength there was left in her little arms, she pushed her father from her brother. The woodcutter stumbled on a hearth stone and flung his arms at her to catch his balance. Gretel stepped aside, and he fell headlong toward the oven. At once, Hansel took hold of his father by the back of his breeches and shoved him into the flames. Gretel quickly slammed the oven door and Hansel barred it.

Their faces white with horror, the children stood unmoving by the oven, clamping their fingers to their ears to stop the sound of their father's screams, which went on and on. All the while, the infants howled and from the chimney the flames sent up a blackish, foul-smelling smoke.

ॐ

That afternoon, a neighboring farmer had been driving his pigs to nose for truffles in the woods. When the woodcutter had ridden home to bring the children to the house of his betrothed, he and the farmer passed each other along the way and exchanged pleasantries before each went about his business.

At the edge of the wildwood, the farmer heard shouts from the woodcutter's house and listened with interest to the man's violent rebukes. It appeared his children had committed some serious mischief. The farmer was not surprised at the man's rage, for though he knew the woodcutter to be mild-tempered, all the neighborhood had learned from their stepmother of the children's earlier escapade, when they abandoned their father and new mother to labor alone in hard times. It was thought that the brother and sister had returned only because food was again in abundance.

The howls, shouts and cries coming from the cottage assured the farmer that the woodcutter had been driven to chasten his wayward son and daughter at last. The farmer felt some satisfaction at being blessed with obedient offspring.

But when the shrieks issuing from the house continued for some time, and at an unnaturally high pitch, he thought it best to intercede in a neighborly way, to stay the father's rod, for surely the woodcutter would not wish to beat his children to death in a fit of unregulated anger.

And so it was that the farmer entered the woodcutter's

cottage and came upon a scene: the brother and sister at the barred oven door, covering their ears against the screams of their father trapped inside.

By the time the farmer reached the oven and opened the door, it was too late.

Hansel and Gretel were brought before the King's High Court of Justice and convicted of murdering their own father from motives of envy and malice. In consideration of their tender ages—just seven and eight—the judges were merciful. Instead of death, they sentenced the children to imprisonment in the King's dungeons. There they passed their lives amongst villains and scoundrels and murderers awaiting execution as well as many miserable wretches who had stolen bread or killed a brutal master. And oft were the times in the damp and dark of that hopeless place, that Hansel and Gretel did wonder why ever had they sought to escape the wildwood and the expeditious flames of the witch's oven.

NEITHER HERE NOR THERE

"*I never* dreamed of such happiness as this while I was a duckling," exclaimed the young swan. He raised his strong wings and stretched his neck to its full length, then drew it back into the splendid curve he had been so ashamed of when he lived among ducks. No more!

He swam from one end of the pond to the other and back again, uttering *yeeb yeeb yeebs* of delight and bowing to the other swans, who returned his bow respectfully. "These are swans, and I am one of them," he kept repeating to himself as if he could not quite believe it. He padded up the bank and stood surveying his new world. "There on those islets are swans' resting places," he exulted. "And this is swan's down caught here in the brush, and here—" he lifted one foot and shook off some muck "—are swan droppings! Oh the rapture!" The very clouds overhead seemed to take the shape of the great birds. "This is swan sky," he cried, "and swan air."

A family of swans swam into view and he hailed them from the bank. "Good morning! Good morning to you!" They raised their necks in a pleasant greeting and swept serenely past. "These gentle creatures are my relations," he said to himself, overwhelmed by the joy of belonging, "my swan kinsfolk, my swan brothers and sisters!" And he gazed again, for the hundredth time, at his reflection in the pond.

He was in the second year of life. Summer came, and the swans dropped their old feathers. He waited companionably with the others for the time when the whole flock would fly to their winter home. They were courteous and amiable toward him. There was no pecking or chasing. No harassing or taunting or mocking. They greeted one another in tranquil silence. When they spoke, it was with quiet notes low in the throat. If annoyed, they merely hissed.

When their new feathers had grown in, the flock flew to the winter lake. Here, their large paddling feet kept the deep water from freezing over. During the cold nights, the young swan warmed himself with thoughts of a particular female who dipped her bill at him in a coquettish way. It seemed a genteel form of seduction compared to the wing flapping, standing on tails and preening he had observed in flirting ducks. And so he responded in kind, and in early spring they became a pair. He addressed her as 'Coquette'. She, having heard his story, called him, with affectionate irony, 'My Ugly Duckling'.

ᘓ

"Come, My Ugly Duckling," said the lady to her mate on the day after they joined together in a nuptial embrace. "We must now search for a place to build our nest."

The young swan yawned and shook his neck. "What, *both* of us?" he asked. He had been planning to catch minnows for his breakfast.

"Of course, what a question," said Coquette. She arched her wings to stretch them, stepped down from the bank, and swam off at a good pace. Her mate stirred himself and followed, but slowly. When he caught up with her, she was poking around a little island of brush and willows. "How slow you are," she teased him. "Tell me, My Ugly Duckling, what do you think of this for a nesting place?"

"I suppose it's all right," he said. "Here, by the bank, is a bit of grass and brush that you can drop your eggs into. That should do."

"A bit of grass and brush?" replied Coquette. "You are joking, surely." Surveying the shore, she spotted a stand of reeds and cattails near some overhanging willows. "There," she said, swimming swiftly toward them. "Those should serve nicely for the foundation. Let us set to work at once." The young swan was at that moment drifting off to make a breakfast of water striders, but he was brought back sharply by Coquette's hiss of annoyance. "My dear Duckling, what do you mean by dawdling so?"

"Why, I was hungry," he said in surprise at her tone.

"But we must claim our site and begin building upon it before it is taken by another pair. It will be hot work once the sun is high. Come, come. Let us begin. We can eat later." And she began to pull vigorously at a cattail with her bill, uprooting the plant and carrying it to the spot beneath the willow.

"But, I—I am not fit for such work," said her mate. "That is the work of women. Males have nothing to do with it."

"Nothing to do with it?" said Coquette. "What can you mean? Are you not a swan? All swans do this kind of work. Do you intend to behave like a duck?"

He was abashed, for indeed he only knew what he had observed of ducks. "Not at all," he said, and scrambled heartily up the bank in an effort to hide his ignorance. "Cattails, you say?" He broke off a great many of them and a goodly number of other reeds before she could stop him.

"Hold, hold," she said. "Do not destroy the whole cover.

Pick judiciously, and mind what you have taken already," for several of his reeds had fallen from his bill and were floating away.

The building of the nest went poorly. Coquette had to stop her own work often to instruct her mate, who seemed confounded by the requirement of arranging the sticks and weeds into an orderly platform. At first he felt anxious lest anyone else observe him at this female labor, but glancing across the pond he noticed other males helping their mates construct identical platforms, except that their work was going faster apace than his. Now he was ashamed of his efforts and blustered, "Why all this fuss? A small hollow in the grass serves well enough for a few eggs," and under his breath grumbled, "and what is the sense of *my* being involved?"

But at last the platform was built and a downy nest ensconced in it with four eggs laid snugly within. These were all of a strange blue-green color the likes of which the young swan had never seen in an egg. But he was not much interested in them, looking forward now to a period of leisure with his fellows while his lady sat upon her brood. He started to swim away.

Coquette called after him. "I would like shellfish, some lily roots, a tadpole or two, and a small worm if you can find one, my dear, and please don't be long. I am famished."

The young swan stopped paddling and turned to stare at her. "What?!" said he. "You expect me to bring you food?"

"Why of course. Unless you would rather take your turn now sitting upon these eggs and have me bring supper to you."

"Take my turn?!" he said incredulously. "Why ever should such a thing be necessary? Just scratch some feathers and grass over them. That will keep them warm enough. Then come and find your own food."

"The idea!" Coquette snorted at him. "Why, such a practice would kill them in their shells."

"Perhaps three or four of them, but the other six or eight would likely survive."

"Good heavens, do you imagine I am sitting on such an outlandish quantity of eggs? Do you forget that I laid only four?"

"How could I know that you stopped at four," he said, defensively, "when the customary number is eight or ten, or even twelve?"

"Customary number!" she hissed, opening her wings and rising from the nest before calming herself and settling down again in an effort at patience. "What a notion. And how callous you are about the fate of your children. It is positively unfatherly. Why, each egg is as precious as the other, as any natural swan will tell you."

The young swan swam off peevishly and stayed away until he had eaten his fill of fish and insects. Then, seeing the other males hurrying back to their nests with tidbits in their bills for their mates, he plucked a dragonfly from the air and swam back to present it to Coquette. She swallowed the insect in one gulp and, rising to her feet, stepped from the nest in a huff. "Come," said she. "*You* sit on these eggs while I get myself a *proper* meal." And with that she plopped into the water with an angry splash and swam away.

He could not believe his ears. "Sit on eggs!" he thought. "It is absurd." But, as all the other male swans were engaged in helping their mates, and depriving him of comradeship, there was nothing else for him to do. Unless he wanted to swim foolishly alone, he must sit on the eggs, which he did at last, though he found the task uncomfortable and tiresome.

ى

Coquette and he made little conversation during the rare times they spent at the nest together. This general silence of swans had begun to unnerve him. "Are you all mute?" he accused her. "Have swans no skill of conversation?" To which she replied in her quiet voice, "I should prefer to remain silent all the day long than make that dreadful '*yeeb, yeeb, yeeb*' sound that you utter incessantly. Whatever can you mean by it? I never heard a swan engage in such meaningless patter."

The cygnets stayed unhatched for an interminable spell. On the twenty-fifth day, the young swan listened for the taps and pecks of hatching infants, but in vain. When twenty-seven days had come and gone, he declared to Coquette philosophically, "Well, my dear, they must be dead. There's really no reason to continue this endeavor." She struck him a smart whack with her wing and said, "Do not pretend ignorance just to shirk your duty. There are ten more days to wait, as you well know."

But he had not known, and now the knowledge dismayed him. "Why must swans drag out this tedious business to veritable infinity? It is abnormal and inefficient."

Whenever it was his turn to be off the nest, he stayed away for as long as he dared, attempting again to engage the other males in amusement and banter. But they only looked down their bills at him, and once he overheard one of them whisper discreetly to another, "That's the swan who was raised by ducks, you know," to which his companion nodded sagely. "Ah, that explains it then. One can't really blame the poor fellow. They see things quite differently from us."

"Swans..." said the young swan to himself, "why, the whole lot are priggish!" He tried to waylay another male, bent on his errands, but was politely rebuffed. "Swans have no idea of society," he observed. "They are preoccupied from morning to night with work and duty and haven't the least notion of camaraderie or fun. And that's to say nothing of this unnatural closeness between males and females. I would not have believed it if I had not experienced it."

The cygnets hatched on the thirty-sixth day.

"Help *care* for them?!" the young swan protested. "But they are hatched now. What should I do for them but be in their way? It is the mother to whom they must grow attached." But no, he was expected to swim about in close attendance to the brood of four along with Coquette as if this were the most ordinary occurrence in the world.

"The children must never be left alone, for they cannot fly from enemies," said his mate. But he saw no reason why *he* should protect them. Coquette was fully able to do so. Besides, the backward, ungainly little cygnets refused even to try their wings.

"How they do lag about us day in and day out. If they were left to their own devices, they would sprout wing feathers and fly soon enough," thought the young swan, the humiliation of his own delayed flight lost in the dimness of infant memory. "Why, these cygnets are fully *twice* as old as ducklings are when *they* first take wing. Look at the great awkward things. They ride upon their mother's back the moment they grow a little tired. They hide away in her feathers as soon as the temperature turns cool. I have to pull out water plants the livelong day to feed them." He concluded that swan children were unhealthily coddled. They could learn a good deal from a single day of care by a duck mother, that was certain.

The time came, many weeks later, when the cygnets did at last learn to fly and could look after themselves. The Ugly Duckling and Coquette shed their old feathers and grew strong new ones. The young swan looked to the sky eagerly and said, "Now I shall return to the winter lake and have a good rest."

Coquette stared at him. "I can't have heard you right," said she. "I thought you said '*I*'. Surely you mean '*we*', for I shall be going too."

"Of course you will," said he, "and I am certain you will enjoy your holiday there as much as I will mine." He began to beat the air with his great wings in preparation for flight. "Good-bye," he called to her over the rush of wind. "I cannot say I enjoyed our months together, but I am hopeful that my succeeding mates will be more liberal in their views."

"'*Succeeding mates!*'" she hissed. "I am your wife! Swan husbands and wives do not part in their lifetime." But he was already circling to the south, leaving her gaping up at him as if he were a creature of an alien species.

ॐ

At the winter lake, the young swan was struck again by the silence of his kinsfolk. None spoke with more than a low grunt or quiet snort or an occasional hiss. Nowhere on the lake did he find the loud and lively bustle one expected of a great migrating flock in autumn. Where were the brassy, hilarious quacks of the females, the reedy '*yeeb, yeeb, yeeb*' of the males, the flutter and flap and splash of arguing, competing, and struggling birds in the throes of life?

He swam among the mute swans lonely and disdainful. Yes, they had beauty of a kind, he admitted, but he was beginning to regard their long curved necks as somewhat grotesque and their white plumage as unvaryingly, *monotonously* white. Where were the necks of iridescent green, the metallic, purplish-blue wing patches of the male, the tawny browns and beiges that so distinguished the female?

Just then a flock of ducks wearing these very colors passed overhead on their way to another, different watering place, and he remembered his foster mother—the one who had raised him—how she had praised his good disposition and defended his swimming against the criticism of others, though she had to concede his ugliness. Now he felt a queer longing for home, although the swans' winter lake *was* home. But then he remembered how he had been bitten and pecked and pushed about and ridiculed by the ducks and kicked at by the farmer lass and nearly shot by hunters, and he knew he could not return to his old life.

"I am neither here nor there," he mourned, swimming alone in circles on the vast lake, politely shunned by the other swans, who, by this time, had all heard of his betrayal of his wife and his shocking indifference toward his offspring.

The whole winter long, he paddled about in isolation, coming eventually to float listlessly alone for hours on out-of-the-way inlets. "What does it matter if my feet are caught in the ice?" thought he. "It is as good a way to die as any." He barely looked at his reflection in the water now, for when he caught a glimpse of it, he no longer had any clear idea what he ought to look like. When the snow fell on his back, he didn't bother to shake it off. Soon he came to resemble a lonely little iceberg in the middle of the lake.

When the spring breezes began to blow warm and the swans dipped their bills and swung their heads at each other and paired off and flew away, the young swan stayed behind alone. He swam aimlessly from one shore to the other. At night he tucked his bill into his feathers and fell into a troubled sleep.

One morning just at dawn, he was wakened by a single, plaintive *quack*. He raised his neck and looked to the sky for the sight of ducks passing over, but none were to be seen. The quack came again, from far across the lake. He scanned the distant shore. Then, from a hidden inlet, a small creature rounded the peninsula. She swam alone and erratically, her wake fanning out in a crooked pattern behind her. "Quack," she cried tremulously and "quack" again. She was swimming in his direction, and as she came, he saw that she was much larger than she had appeared from afar. She held her wings high like sails and had a long, curved, graceful neck. She was, in fact, a young swan like himself, but one he had never seen on the lake before, a stranger. The newcomer came on hesitantly, pausing at intervals to look down at herself in the water, then up at him, and down at herself again. Then, seemingly reassured, she uttered another timid, hopeful quack.

THE MAGIC LOOKING GLASS

Once upon a time, there was a headstrong little Princess. Her parents, the King and Queen, hired one nurse after another, but none was capable of governing her. Whenever the nurse's back was turned, the little Princess climbed the stairs to the tower and stood balancing upon the parapets, or she descended to the kitchens and tasted the butter still in the churns, or she slipped away to visit the befouled barnyard animals in their sties and pens. Once, just before a visiting monarch was to be shown the royal gardens, she picked all the roses and presented them to the kitchen maids.

If the truth be told, the King and Queen took little interest in their child, except to bemoan her unruliness and lack of decorum. "If only she would behave as a princess ought," complained the King, "we could get on with pressing matters of the realm and not be continually distracted."

"Yes," lamented the Queen, "it pushes ones patience to the limit."

It so happened that an avaricious and cunning sorcerer heard of their plight and presented himself at the castle. He brought along a large wooden crate which, when carried into the great hall and prized open, revealed an ornate looking-glass. The magician explained that this was a magic looking-glass which would reflect whatever one wished to see—not only the image of oneself, but of all the world and beyond. "The mirror always tells the truth," added the sorcerer.

"It is a wonderful device, indeed," said the Queen, "but what has it to do with our wayward daughter?"

"When once she looks into the mirror and beholds its entrancing visions, nothing else will interest her, and, without urging, she will curtail her frolicking."

"That would be a fine solution, if it were possible," said the King, "but I doubt even magic can put an end to the child's escapades."

"I shall leave the mirror with you for seven days," said the sorcerer. "Put it in the girl's chamber and watch what happens. If you are not satisfied, I shall take it away again. But if it serves you as I have predicted, I will sell you the looking-glass for a thousand gold ingots."

The King and Queen were rather taken aback by so high a price, but thought there would be nothing lost by giving the mirror a try. Forthwith, the looking-glass was placed in the little girl's room. "Look into it, child," said her mother, "and whatever you wish to see will be shown you." The girl ran to the mirror and said, "I want to see cook's spaniel!" The creature had died of old age not ten days before, and the Princess had been very fond of it. Suddenly, there in the mirror appeared the dear old fellow, its ears just as loppy and soft-looking as ever. The child gazed at the image tenderly, then, prancing with pleasure, asked, "May I really see whatever I want?"

"Yes, but only if you promise to behave."

"I wish to see the back of myself!" said the Princess, and instantly the mirror revealed the wisps of auburn hair curling at the nape of her neck and an indigo stain on the hem of her dress where she had dipped it in a dyeing vat to see the effect of blueing on white satin. "I can see myself coming and going!" she exclaimed.

So the magic mirror was placed in her chamber, and the King and Queen were hopeful of its beneficial effect.

But the next morning they were wakened by a commotion as usual. In the yard below, the cook and her assistants were dashing about trying to retrieve a basketful of down feathers plucked from a recently killed goose. The feathers had been saved for comforters and pillows, but the little Princess had discovered the basket, tipped it over, and was flinging the goosedown into the air for the pleasure of watching it float away on the breeze.

"There, you see!" said the King to his wife. "Nothing will make that child behave. She is incorrigible!"

But the Queen urged him to be patient. "Remember," said she, "that the sorcerer has given the mirror seven days to work its magic." She hurried down to the courtyard, seized her daughter by the arm and ordered her to come inside and play with the looking-glass. But the little Princess was entranced with the flurry of summertime snow she had launched into the air. She slipped from her mother's grasp and raced away. Her mother exhorted her, running close behind, "Wouldn't you like to see *fairies* flying instead?"

This stopped the child at once. "Oh yes!" said she.

"Go and ask the magic looking-glass to show you them." And the child scampered into the castle and disappeared into her chamber.

The fairies in the magic mirror swooped and soared and fluttered in the air like hummingbirds. The Princess watched them in awed silence a full half hour before becoming restless. Then she jumped up and pulled the silk curtains from around her little bed and ran out of the room and down to the great hall. With the draperies streaming out behind her, she burst into the throne room where the King and Queen were holding court. "Here are my wings!" she cried, her cheeks ablaze with eagerness. "I am a fairy, too!" The King glowered, and thundered at an attendant to remove her.

"Well, well," sighed the Queen. "The girl was quiet for a *while* at least."

The next morning, the little Princess rose from her bed and went to stand before her magic mirror. "Show me an elephant from the Indies," said she, for her nurse had told her all about elephants and she had been dreaming of them. There in the glass appeared a leviathan, lumbering through a savanna. Its baby followed behind, the little trunk curled around the mother's tail. The Princess was surprised when she placed her hand on the mirror, to find only smooth glass and not the leathery hide of the great animal.

She was summoned to breakfast just then, and, pretending to be an elephant, lumbered down the stairs on all fours until she misstepped and tumbled to the bottom, bruising her knees and scraping her hands on the flagstones. Before she was allowed her strawberries and cream, she had to be scolded and have fingers shaken at her and her wounds seen to. But she soon forgot these, for she spied a dead lark on the terrace and spent the rest of the morning giving the decaying bird a ceremonious funeral.

"How you do reek!" her father complained. He ordered the maids to wash her and afterward take her to her magic looking-glass and bid her play with it. A grand banquet was planned for the evening and he hoped to prevent her crawling under the tables and tickling the guests' ankles or getting into some other mischief.

"Show me my dead lark in heaven," said the Princess to the mirror. The glass was at once suffused with a golden celestial light, and the lark, its wings spread wide and its head framed by a halo, soared above the clouds. The Princess spent the rest of the evening requesting one image after another until her eyelids drooped and she fell asleep on the carpet in front of the mirror.

The next morning she woke stiff and tired at the foot of the looking-glass and stared into it dully. "What shall I do today?" she wondered aloud and at once saw in the mirror her own person on the back of a little donkey climbing to the top of a snow-capped peak, where she dismounted and frolicked in the snow. She sat for an hour watching herself until a maid had to draw her away by the hand to be dressed and given her breakfast.

For the next four days, she returned to the looking-glass more and more often until, as the sorcerer promised, she spent so many hours in front of it that there was no time left for mischief. Whenever her parents found her sitting before the mirror, they would creep away, half expecting on their return to find she had scampered off as before, but, no, there she would still be sitting as if she had not moved an inch from her little couch. Her head would be tilted forward, her eyes unblinking, her hands in her lap, and her feet set together in the manner her governess had unsuccessfully tried to make her sit for lessons. The King and Queen had never seen the child so harmlessly occupied and so becalmed.

They did not wait for the week to be out before paying the sorcerer his thousand ingots but instead called him back the very next day. He bade them have the gold piled on a great wagon, and then he rode off with it.

Week upon week the little Princess sat before the looking-glass watching one spectacle after another, anything that popped into her mind—a parade of camels crossing an Arabian desert, a tournament of jousting knights, babies delivered in little bundles in the beaks of storks. She was at the looking-glass the first thing after jumping out of bed every morning and the last thing before being dragged to bed at night. When she was obliged to learn her needlework or practice upon her little lute or take her meals, she would grow restless and irritable and beg to return to her chamber where she could recline on the couch and immerse herself in whatever marvel she had conjured up.

Now when she was made to take exercise in the garden, she wandered about listlessly, for there was nothing very interesting to see. Though the roses were in bloom, she was not tempted to pluck them, nor did she take notice of their fragrance. Though the laundresses had spread the linens on the grass to dry, she had no interest in lying down upon them to breathe their sunlight.

After many months, the day came when the Princess saw and heard so little of the world outside her chamber that she could think of nothing else for the mirror to show her. She grew languid and did not know what to do with herself. In exasperation, she cried aloud, "Looking-glass, is there nothing else to see?" and was startled to hear the mirror reply, "Of course there is! I can show you a great deal!" At this, the Princess sat down upon her couch, expectantly. "And will it all be true, as before?" she asked.

"I always tell the truth," said the mirror.

From then on, the Princess asked the looking-glass to show her whatever it would, while she reclined upon her couch and simply watched, relieved of the necessity to conjure pictures from nursery tales or her own imagination.

⌇

Years passed and the Princess grew to the age of sixteen. Her magic looking-glass had shown her countless sights and events. The riches and opulence of Arab potentates and emperors of Cathay and kings and queens of Africa. The great oceans crashing against the mirror's glass almost as if they might break it and flood the room. Exotic creatures cavorting in the tops of trees that grew in distant climes. Rural bumpkins, whose antics and buffoonery made her laugh. Selfless servants whose acts of loyalty made her cry. A goodly number of events which she might rather not have witnessed—the crushing of peasant rebellions, and the public beheading of their leaders, the burning at the stake of heretics and witches, poisonings and usurpations of monarchs by ambitious uncles and brothers.

But the images that affected her the most and were by far the greatest in number were the legions of beautiful princesses that appeared in the mirror everyday. Each more perfect than the last, these became the young Princess's companions since she had long since ceased to run about the castle, befriending everyone from cooks to counts.

Without exception, the princesses were flawless of form—buxom and slim-waisted, crowned with hair as thick as ermine and fine as thistledown, blessed with limbs both long and graceful. She wondered, as she examined her own reflection anxiously, if she would attain the perfection of the looking-glass princesses when she was grown.

"Am I beautiful?" she often asked the mirror, and the mirror always replied, "Judge for yourself." Compared to the flawless princesses, her own beauty seemed paltry. Her hair was luxuriant, yes, but theirs was sumptuous. Her eyes were thickly lashed, but theirs doubly so. Her feet, though small, were not as dainty. Her bosom and hips, as she grew to womanhood, did not flair with quite so much abundance as theirs, nor did her waist pinch off as narrowly. Now each day she asked the mirror, "Am I yet as beautiful as they?" And the mirror replied as always, "Judge for yourself."

She attended closely to their lives. The beautiful looking-glass princesses were always rescued by brave princes before they could be harmed by wild beasts or wicked men. But the plainer women—the out-of-favor ladies-in-waiting, the serving maids, crones, and peasants—invariably came to tragic ends, rebuffed, ignored, made objects of fun or ravished and cast aside.

Fear came upon the Princess and she began to think of nothing but beauty and how she might enhance her own. "Show me how to be more beautiful, Looking-glass," she pleaded, and the mirror displayed unguents for silkening the skin, potions for reflecting moonlight in the hair, high-heeled slippers for creating the illusion of stature, laces to cinch the waist, deeply cut gowns lined with ivory stays to enhance the cleft of the bosom. "I must have these articles!" she exclaimed to the mirror. "How may I come by them?"

The mirror assured her that anything she required could be obtained from the sorcerer who had sold the magic looking-glass to her parents. She ran to the Queen and King and begged them to buy at once all the items that the mirror had shown her. So the magician was summoned and when he arrived he bowed solicitously and offered his services.

"Perhaps Your Majesties are beset by treacherous rivals and

you are in need of devices for discreetly dispatching them. I can sell you a peck of poisoned apples, or—should the rival be a woman—these elegant laces" —here he drew his cloak half open to reveal many pockets full of wares— "which, when worn, will shrink to the point of cutting off the lady's breath. Or—" he opened the other side of his cloak— "these poisoned combs. Drawn through the lady's hair, they will render her lifeless. Either one will do the deed nicely. Or perhaps you would prefer—"

"Nothing like that," interrupted the King. "We are in need of articles to enhance our daughter's beauty."

"Ah," said the sorcerer. "Of those items I can provide you with a great variety."

"Buy them all, Father," urged the Princess, and the articles were duly exchanged for another thousand ingots—a shocking price—but the King and Queen thought it gold well spent, for it happened that there was a powerful young king in a nearby kingdom, whose queen had died in childbirth, and he was now eligible to marry their daughter. A marriage uniting the two kingdoms would be advantageous to both. A meeting was arranged.

Now, in anticipation of this meeting, the Princess applied fragrant oils to her skin. She combed herbal potions into her hair. She had herself laced until there was hardly any breath left in her body. She fit herself into gowns that clung to her hips and pressed her bosom into the shape of ripe peaches. She wore slippers so pointed and slim that her toes fell asleep and would scarcely hold her upright.

On the morning before she was to be presented to the young king, she asked the magic mirror, "Now am I beautiful enough?"

"Judge for yourself," it replied, and showed her a ballroom full of princesses dancing in the arms of brave princes. She studied each one attentively and then studied her own reflection and thought at last, "Yes, perhaps I am as beautiful as they."

The King arrived. He was a well-formed, handsome man, dignified, yet with a trace of good humor playing about his lips. The Princess at once judged him to be a monarch as noble as those princes who rescued the looking-glass princesses from dragons and villains, and she now drew upon all the arts of enticement she had learned from those young ladies. She assumed an air of combined demureness and coquetry. Willing a maidenly blush to flood her cheeks, she made a deep curtsey, even as she pressed a lace handkerchief to her bosom as if to subdue an unmaidenly rise of passion.

The King was accompanied by a nurse who carried his infant daughter, a charming little cherub with sweet round eyes and cheeks like roses painted upon porcelain. "My child is the light of my life," said he. The Princess, too tightly laced to speak above a whisper, gasped her admiration for the infant, then cast her eyes modestly down.

Struck by her beauty and decorum, the King decided on the spot to make her his wife and the stepmother of his child. And so they were married.

༄

The Princess, now a Queen, ordered her magic looking-glass to be removed from the castle of her childhood to her husband's palace, where it hung in her private chamber. As soon as she was alone, she hurried to it and asked most urgently,

> "Mirror, mirror on the wall,
> Who is the fairest of them all?"

and the mirror replied,

"You are fairest of them all."

And for the first time since the mirror had shown her the beautiful princesses, her mind was at ease.

For two years, the Queen was content. Nurses cared for her little stepdaughter while she and the King attended to their duties. The Queen endured many a banquet and ball in pinching shoes, bruising stays, and tight laces that took her voice away. She restricted herself to the most sedate forms of dancing and on breezy evenings avoided balconies and lawns for fear of disarranging her coiffure. But she was rewarded for her pains. Her husband called her his beautiful bride and smiled upon her proudly as she sat, still and elegant as a statue, even into the wee hours of the morning.

The King's little daughter grew fast and was soon toddling gaily about the palace and its grounds. Her small feet could be heard up and down the stones of the courtyards and upon the garden paths. She was allowed to explore without restraint, for her father could not resist the appeal of the little girl's wide eyes and fair cheeks, the pretty smile on her red lips and the gentle toss of her raven curls. He called her Snow-white.

She was a spirited little Princess, all frisking and fun, and accompanied her father everywhere. She sat beside him at breakfast and played with his crown and pulled his beard without the least interference. Indeed, the King and all the court laughed at her antics and were charmed. Even her nurses chastened her but gently, though she played so often with the guinea hens that they forgot to lay and there were no eggs for breakfast. Once, having slipped into the treasury room, she was found hours later sitting inside a miniature castle she had built from towers of gold coins.

Far from chastising his daughter for her conduct, the King indulged it. To please him, the Queen, too, lavished praise on her stepdaughter and petted and fondled her and declared there had never been such a charming little Princess in legend or in life.

But though she appeared to have affection for her stepdaughter, the young Queen found the child's behavior irritating. That no one cared to subdue the headstrong little girl seemed a dereliction of duty. And the fact that her stepdaughter's pretty face and winsome ways should be the cause of this indulgence made it the more annoying. It galled her to the point of illness to hear others admire the child's face and form so extravagantly. "She is spoiled," thought the Queen.

She kept her complaints to herself and treated Snow-white with the show of affection that a stepmother should, but whenever she took the child on her lap, the girl—who customarily embraced anyone without distinction—grew stiff and sober-eyed and seemed to shrink into herself. The Queen thought, "Her sweetness is a sham. She is cold-hearted, whatever anyone else may think," and within a minute's time would set her stepdaughter back on her feet and feel herself rid of an odious burden.

Snow-white grew into a tall, graceful child, so lovely that people stopped their occupation to gaze upon her whenever she passed. Yet she seemed entirely unconscious of the impression she made. She endured her nurse's pains to adorn her hair or dress her in jeweled gowns, but seldom looked at herself in mirrors, and although she returned polite thanks to those who praised her beauty, she betrayed no self-consciousness on the subject.

When the girl was but seven years old, the Queen had

a dreadful shock. One day, she asked her looking-glass the question, as usual:

> "Mirror, mirror on the wall,
> Who is the fairest of them all?"

and the mirror answered,

> "Queen, you are full fair, 'tis true
> But Snow-white fairer is than you."

For some minutes, the Queen stared at the mirror in disbelief. Then she noticed the horrified countenance it gave back to her. She struggled to soften the grim expression hardening her features, but the smile she tried to affect resembled the snarl of a dog under attack. Her eyes were bitter. She could not look at herself for long.

As soon as she turned away from her reflection, she was overcome with weeping. All the afternoon she wept as if her heart would break, though she could not fathom why she should be so affected.

༉

The next day, the Queen saw her stepdaughter set her embroidery hoop carelessly aside and run off to climb the high garden wall. The girl walked the narrow length of it, balancing precariously and almost tumbling off several times. Then she climbed down into the garden and plucked a bushelful of just-opening gardenias, which she carried to the stables to feed to the horses. A queer sensation constricted the Queen's throat as she watched these antics, an unaccountable catch and throb, as if she might shed tears of sadness. But for what? As quickly as it came, the sensation left her, replaced by sour resentment. It seemed to the Queen that she had never known a more selfish, heedless or rebellious girl. Later in the afternoon, she saw Snow-white push open the door of the chamber where the King was closeted with his ministers, debating a grave matter of the realm. The King looked up, frowning at the interruption, then seeing the source of it, held his arms out wide, his frown dissolving into a smile of pleasure. At this, the Queen turned away, unable to tolerate the spectacle.

That evening, she took her meal alone in her chamber but had no appetite. When she turned to the looking-glass for distraction, it showed the banquet hall below and the child beside her father's chair, sharing his plate of grapes. The Queen abruptly turned the looking-glass to the wall.

She went to her dressing table and for some time studied herself in an ordinary mirror. After a while, she rose and loosened her stays and laces, pulled her hair from its pins and let it hang in disheveled locks. Then she lay down upon her couch and slept fitfully until midnight, dreaming of a stunted, misshapen orphan who scuttled among the legs of dancing princesses, tripping them up and causing them to curse and kick at her. The Queen woke feeling wan and ill. She rose and turned her looking-glass back around to face her. Once again she asked, "Who is the fairest of all?" though she had no doubt of the answer.

The mirror showed her the little Snow-white asleep in her bed, her lips parted in a dreaming smile, her hair tumbled around her angelic face. The Queen stared at the hateful image for a long time, and then brought her face closer to examine it more intimately.

The moon had passed from behind a cloud, sending a shaft of light upon the sleeping face. As the Queen watched, the ruby lips in the mirror turned as red as blood, the dark tresses black as ebony. All color drained from the porcelain cheek, leaving it as white as snow. The child appeared unearthly, like an apparition, and the Queen put a hand to the glass as if to test the chill of the sleeping girl's flesh. The glass was as cold as the grave.

The Queen shuddered. "The child is a vixen!" she cried aloud, though there was no one in the room to hear but the looking-glass. "Their angelic darling! She tricks them all—" Her voice was trembling and shrill. And now she saw what it was she must do.

She ran to the outer chamber and called for her maids to bathe and lace and coif her. She chose a gown of emerald green, to set off her auburn hair. She bit her lips to redden them.

Then she dismissed the maids, bidding them to send for a huntsman. The man came without delay and stood humbly at her chamber door. Cap in hand, he could only stammer a greeting. He looked down at his boots, then up, and down and up again, as if stealing glances at her. Taking resolve from the man's admiration, the Queen informed him of his duty.

When he realized the nature of the task demanded of him, he dropped his cap, forgot himself, and stared boldly into her eyes. "Not the lovely little Princess!" he blurted. He fell to his knees before the Queen and implored her, "Your Highness, I beg you not to hold me to such a charge! Snow-white is a sweet child, beloved by all!"

"You will kill her and do it without delay," commanded the Queen. "I order it."

"Then if I must slay an innocent," the huntsman pleaded, miserably, "let it at least be one who is malformed or homely. I shall never be able to look upon her exquisite face and do the deed."

At these words the Queen's eyes blazed like burning coals. She stood over the kneeling huntsman and stared down at him with a smile so cruel in such a beautiful face that he flung his hands up as if to repel a blow. She said, her voice as cold as ice, "Huntsman, on pain of death, you will slay Snow-white and no other." Her lip curled in a callous sneer. "And when you finish the act, you will cut out her heart and bring it to me on the point of your blade." With these words, she dismissed him.

Instead of retiring to her inner chamber where she might stare at the morning's visions revealed in her mirror, as was her custom, she ascended to the tower. From the parapets she watched the sun come up over field and forest, hill and valley. It sparkled on the river that wound through them. But the Queen did not relish this unsurpassed view, for she found herself remembering old scenes framed in the looking-glass. Scenes of betrayings and poisonings and beheadings. Only when she saw out of the corner of her eye two far-away figures crossing the meadow below did the Queen's mind return to the present. It was the huntsman leading Snow-white by the hand toward the woods. The two little figures walked slowly under the canopy of trees and disappeared beneath them.

A short moan, abbreviated by her tight lacing, escaped the Queen. She gripped the stones of the wall and peered intently at the spot where the two had entered the forest.

"How soon will the act take place?" she wondered. "Perhaps the man will do it the moment they are out of sight and she walks a little ahead of him or when she stoops to pick a flower. He will unsheathe his knife and strike her from behind to avoid a glimpse of her trusting expression." Her knuckles whitened on the cold stone. "But perhaps, just at the moment he raises his knife, she will scamper off on some frolic or other and he will have to give chase." Bitterness rose in her throat as she thought of the child's frolicsomeness and how indulgently it was encouraged by the King.

"What else could I have done?" she whispered. "With such a headstrong girl as that, one who would grow to be as willful and treacherous a woman as she is a child—" the Queen clutched the parapet almost as if she might throw herself off "—what other course remains in such a case but to put the child away and cut out her heart?"

A TRUE PRINCESS

The Princess, with regal carriage, entered the royal bed chamber. Her wedding dress of white silk damask glittered with a thousand diamonds. The Prince felt quite dizzy at the sight of her and had to grasp the bedpost to keep from being overcome by emotion.

"My precious dove," he said, "I swore a solemn oath to God that I would not wed until He sent me a real princess of true aristocratic bearing, as my parents so keenly desired, and that, should He grant my wish, I would be faithful to her always and seek no other. Nor will there ever be an oath so easily kept as this one. You are indeed the true princess I have sought, and in that gown, you are a celestial being that Heaven's angels themselves must envy."

"My treasured husband," replied the Princess, breathlessly, "please overlook my unbecoming boldness if I beg to divest myself of this gown at once. Every jewel-encrusted yard of it weighs upon my flesh, which longs for the caress of gentle air."

To the Prince's astonishment and delight, she slowly and with graceful movements untied each ribbon one by one along the bodice, allowing the dress to slide around her hips and fall to the floor until she stood in only the softest, most pellucid of clinging undergarments, which by candlelight revealed the contour of her regal figure. She breathed a voluptuous sigh. "Ah, my lord, you cannot know what exquisite release this brings me."

He crossed the room and took her in his arms. "My royal darling," he murmured into her thick black tresses. "When I heard that you could not sleep for the torment of a single pea beneath twenty mattresses and twenty feather beds, I knew you then for a true princess, though you had come to the palace door as bedraggled, in the rain, as an urchin. An urchin!" He chuckled at the irony of it, but his laugh turned husky with passion and he kissed her fervently. She went limp in his arms as if she, too, were so affected by the strength of her ardor that she might faint.

Then, withdrawing a little, she pressed her delicate fingers to his chest. "My precious," she said, "the stench of your breath is so putrid I fear I shall swoon from it."

"What did you say?" He did not think he heard her right.

"I am afraid your breath will make me ill."

He drew back, aghast. "How can that be? For two days I have refrained from taking meat or cheese or fish or wine. I ate only fruit at the wedding banquet and cleansed my mouth with *eau de lavandre* in anticipation of our night of bliss!"

"Nonetheless, there linger traces of cabbage—"

"—consumed a week ago!" interrupted the Prince.

"—And Brie—"

"Last month! When the French ambassador visited and brought it as a gift."

"I beg of you, my sweet, to use a pitcher more of lavender water and try to cleanse your breath again. I am becoming quite flushed with nausea." And she opened the throat of her gossamer chemise to fan her hot flesh, revealing a full and rosy bosom. On seeing this, the Prince hurried to the door to do her bidding. The Princess called after him. "Perhaps a purgative might help as well," she said. "But please take it in a distant part of the palace where the ensuing odor may not reach me." She frowned. "On second thought, best not to purge at all. The smell would find me, no matter where you contrived to do it." So the Prince hurried to the outer chamber and cleansed his mouth four, five, and six times more.

When he returned, the Princess was reclined, entirely disrobed, upon the bed. At once, the Prince joined her there, but had scarcely drawn close to embrace her when she said, "My lamb, do you notice how very hot the room is? It is like a smith's furnace. I am positively feverish from the intensity of it."

The Prince was astounded. "Hot?" he said, taking her hand, which seemed as cool as his. "But it is a perfect June night, as balmy and fresh as one could wish."

"There is but one tolerable temperature," said the Princess, "neither too hot nor too cold but exactly at the point in between—not half a degree more or less—that is most conducive to atmospheric comfort. Perhaps if you opened the casement an inch, a slight breeze would bring the temperature into balance.

"Willingly!" said the Prince, hopping from the bed. "Nothing easier!" and swiftly he opened the window.

"No wider than that!" the Princess warned, too late. He had already opened it a full two inches. Instantly she dove beneath the covers and huddled there. Her muffled voice reproved him. "'One inch only,' I said! Now it is as frigid in the room as an ice palace in deepest winter! Oh, I freeze! I freeze! It will be an hour or more before I am thawed sufficiently to keep my teeth from chattering and my limbs from shivering."

The Prince was at once remorseful. "Forgive me, my delicate darling. I am most sorry for my error. In love's passion I forgot that you are subject to the acute sensibilities of a true princess." He closed the window to an inch and approached the bed.

There was a moving and shifting under the blankets. From beneath them, the Princess sighed. "These coarse coverings chafe so," she said, "but I must stay wrapped or I shall freeze."

"My precious, the bed clothes are of the softest cashmere," the Prince replied, "lined with fine silk and filled with eiderdown. Is it possible they chafe?"

"Oh please do not concern yourself, my dear husband. You have been most solicitous. I shall try to endure it until I am warmer."

Encouraged by her forgiving tone, the Prince answered, "I will hasten the process!" and quickly undressed and slid beneath the covers, taking pains not to expose her to the offending air. "Allow me to warm you," he said. Her skin was silken and creamy to his hot hands, which could not forbear from stroking and fondling her. Under his caress her bosom heaved and her breaths came short and gasping. This pleasure that she exhibited at his touch set his heart to beating violently. He moaned, "Sweet angel, my eagerness has only been heightened—if that can be—by the small delays you have imposed upon us."

He bent to kiss her again, but she pushed him away suddenly, crying out in horror, "Merciful heaven! What horny calluses you have! I feel as if I were pawed by the hooves of a goat! Your fingertips will wear the very flesh off my bones!" The Prince drew back, confounded, and the Princess gasped at the icy breeze his abrupt withdrawal let into the bed. She snatched the blankets more closely around her.

"Calluses!" protested the Prince. "But, my dove, these

hands have never done a moment's worth of labor, except when I have practiced archery or ridden to hounds, and even then I have always worn gloves of double-layered kid. The only task I do bare-handed is to pen a letter or put my name to court documents."

The Princess quizzed him earnestly. "How often does it happen that a quill will split while you are writing?"

"Why, once or twice a twelvemonth, at most."

"That explains it, then. The broken edge of a goose quill will toughen the softest hand. I recommend that you write with swans' quills only, for they are more durable. Call for a pumice stone," she said. "I will smooth your fingertips myself." But when the pumice stone was brought and the Princess, bundled for warmth in layers of eiderdown, began to rub it lightly over the Prince's fingertips, in seconds the task proved too taxing for her dainty hands, and she relinquished it to the attendant, though she oversaw the job vigilantly, not allowing the servant to cease his efforts until an hour had passed.

"A little better," she pronounced, cautiously running a finger over the Prince's reddened fingertips. "Not completely smooth, but perhaps I can bear their touch for brief intervals." By now, the room had warmed to a degree the Princess could tolerate. She dismissed the servant and beckoned the Prince to join her again in bed.

"My noble sovereign," she whispered.

"My sweet," he murmured, nuzzling her neck, "think of the princely heir we shall now commence in creating."

"Oh, my treasure," said she, "I long to do so." Her eyelids fluttered closed as she lay back upon the bed and with charming bashfulness whispered, "Though I am uncertain how it is accomplished."

"Indeed, my little lamb, in your sheltered innocence you

could not guess the particulars, but I shall teach you how it is done, in the tenderest lesson that a pupil could take from any master, so that you will never wish for school to end." The Prince, slender, strong and handsome, took her in his arms and with delicacy and sensitivity, softly rolled with her as if the two of them were logs floating upon the swells of a tranquil lake. She thus sank under him a little way into the billows of fluffy eiderdown.

"Good God!" she cried in a strangled voice. "Your enormous weight crushes my bones as if an earthquake had dropped the battlements upon me! Help! Help! I cannot breathe!" The Prince rolled away immediately and lay beside her, panting with alarm and desire. The Princess chided him severely, "I pray you, husband, take care! My ribs, by no means excessively fragile, were certainly never built to withstand such weight. They are not Grecian columns, to bear the whole tonnage of an Athenaeum roof."

It was a full hour before she had recuperated from the crushing. The Prince, in a state, alternately of excitement and frustration, lay beside her, gingerly holding her hand. At last, she turned with softened eyes and blew a kiss in his direction. "Now, my lord," she said, with chaste and innocent candor, "the lesson you spoke of earlier and so appealingly? I am ready to learn it." Springing to his hands and knees, the Prince mounted her thus, and from such position stretched to his full length above her, supporting himself on bent arms, straightened legs and flexed toes.

"My cherub," he said, "I will require your assistance, if you would be so kind, since my hands, to spare you my weight, are occupied in sustaining the slight gap between us." And he told her what to do, which instructions she followed readily.

The candles had burned to their wicks by now, and the

velvet arm of darkness took the royal couple in its embrace. With the greatest subtlety, almost holding his breath now for fear of discomfiting his bride, the Prince began to project himself forward by inches, at the pace of an ardent, yet patient, snail. "I'm told," he warned her, kindly, "that it hurts a little, just the first time. A pleasant hurt, they say, and soon ended, but I will stop and wait upon your signal, should you feel the slightest twinge. You have only to stay me with your hand."

"Pray do not be anxious on my account, precious darling," said the Princess, in a soft and dreamy voice. "I am not a glass doll that will shatter." She stroked the satiny sheath of her husband's stout wand, then held it fast in her hand as if it were an impetuous bird, that might injure itself beating its wings against her fingers. The Prince continued his forward movement, immeasurably slow, supporting himself by his archer's arms and rider's thighs and toes, which, though strong, trembled now from exertion.

"You must not imagine I am fragile," the Princess assured him. "Of all my sisters, I am the hardiest and least sensitive, as they will attest. Besides," she said, her voice as sensual as a dove's, "how can the clasp of love bring anything but ecstasy?"

At these words, the Prince's passion conspired with the tremor that was beginning to consume his fatiguing limbs. A sudden spasm shook his body and thrust his impetuous bird, still in the Princess's grasp, a full quarter inch into the threshold of its cage.

ॐ

The intermingled screams that echoed down all the palace corridors woke ladies, lords, chambermaids and stewards from the deep slumber that comes before dawn.

A visiting duchess and her coachman started up from their

sleepy embrace, guiltily confusing the screams with alarms of discovery. Various noble children, in a distant wing of the castle cried out in terror at the ghoulish sounds and sobbed for their nursemaids.

The old King and Queen—the Prince's father and mother—woke, too, though both were hard of hearing. The resonating screeches struck them as extreme even for the expression of passionate release that was to be anticipated on a wedding night. The degree and duration of the sounds, coming as they did from the throats of not just one but both participants, boded either very well or very ill for the marriage bed. However, the aged monarchs knew their son's bride to be a true princess, and took the formidable shrieks as a favorable sign, one that presaged the timely production of a royal heir.

So they breathed contented sighs, pulled their bed caps over their ears, and went back to sleep, entwined together companionably like two old cats.

THE GIANT'S LAIR

There, as before, sat the house at the end of the dusty, untraveled road. In five minutes Jack reached it and entered through the gate. The giant's wife was nowhere to be seen, but shirts and breeches as big as ship's sails billowed on a clothesline. At an open window a curtain fluttered. A face moved behind it. He approached the great door and knocked one, two, three times.

"Mistress," he called, "'Tis I, Jack." After a long wait he heard the latch being lifted. The heavy door opened a few inches, and the kindly, careworn face of the giant's wife appeared from behind it.

"Who calls?" said she in a tremulous voice. "My husband is not at home and I do not receive visitors."

"Your husband?" Jack blurted in surprise. "But your husband is dead!"

"My first one, yes," said the giant's wife, "but I speak of my second husband, his brother." She cast a fearful glance down the road. Jack, too, looked back. He turned again to the woman and tipped his hat.

"Good mistress," said he, "you do not remember me. I am the boy, Jack, whom you fed and hid, and who paid you poorly for your kindness by taking your husband's treasures and his life."

The woman looked upon him wonderingly, for he was such a man now as to be unrecognizable. "You are that boy?"

"I am," said he. "And I beg your forgiveness. I was a heedless lad, thinking only of my own poor mother and never considering the consequence to you of my actions." Remorsefully, he explained to her how he had traded his mother's only cow for magic beans, how a beanstalk had grown, as tall as the sky, and how he had climbed the prodigious vine and stolen the giant's treasures—his gold coins and magic hen and singing harp—then descended with his spoils and chopped the beanstalk down, slaying the pursuing giant.

"I thought he must have perished," said she, tonelessly, "when I heard the dreadful howl and crash. I ran down the road, but saw nothing. Then he came no more. But I did not understand how he had met his death."

"The top of the beanstalk hid just beneath the misty bog," Jack told her, pointing toward the distant marsh from which he had come. Over it there hung a low-lying vapor. "And so it does again." The woman shaded her eyes to make out the beanstalk, but as Jack had said, its top was hidden inside the mist.

"How can you have climbed the beanstalk again if it was felled?" she asked.

"I saved a bean," said Jack, "and planted it."

The giant's wife opened the door wider and beckoned Jack to enter. "Come in, young man, for I cannot come out if my husband is not at home. You may stay only a few moments, however, lest he return, find you here, and kill us both."

The kitchen was as tidy and scrubbed as when Jack saw it last and was still decorated with the pleasant touches of a careful, devoted housewife. Boxes of flowers sat in the windowsills, herbs tied with ribbon hung from the rafters, fragrant mince pies cooled on the table. A curly-tailed dog hung about the woman's skirts.

As before, the giant's wife pressed food and drink upon Jack, who, not wanting to offend her, accepted it, though he was loath to take more kindness from one he had so wronged.

"How goes it with you, good mistress?" Jack inquired. "Have you suffered because of my selfish actions?" The woman stared into the stone hearth before speaking.

"After my first husband died, I had no means of making my living and only scraped by, yet I lived content for many months." She hung her head. "It is shameful to find peace at the death of one's husband, yet peaceful I was and even happy. I cannot deny it. I became acquainted with my neighbors and was not so lonely.

"Then my husband's brother, also a giant, arrived at my door. Though he was disappointed to find his brother's wealth stolen by thieves, the house was to his liking, well-proportioned for a giant's comforts. He approved the orderly way I kept it. He paid me compliments and brought me gifts. 'You are lonely here and need protection,' he said. 'The thieves may return and harm you as they did my brother.'"

Shame-faced, the giant's wife said, "I could not tell him that his mighty brother was defeated by a slip of a boy whom I let into his house against his strict orders." Hearing this, Jack's ears turned red from guilt but also pride.

"Once we were married," the woman continued, "my new husband stayed away from home many days at a time, for he is an adventurer who must always be roaming. He likes to conquer uncharted seas, unknown lands, and unclimbed peaks and pinnacles. He is also a suspicious man and forbids me to go out when he is absent." She stared into her hands bleakly. "And hasn't he the right to his suspicions? Did I not deceive my first husband by hiding you, and thus bringing on his death? I have much to atone for."

She sighed. "Now life is lonelier than ever, though I cannot say I enjoy my husband's company when he is at home."

Jack exclaimed, "I will bring back your singing harp, and you shall have its sweet music to comfort your days!"

"Nay, dear boy," replied the giant's wife sadly. "I cannot take it, for my husband would think I had hidden it all the while, denying him its pleasure. He would certainly beat me."

"Then take this gift," said Jack, placing a bag upon the table. When he drew the string, golden eggs spilled out. "You may have as many more as you like."

"Alas," said the woman, "Where would I spend this gold? My husband allows me to go no farther than my front garden."

Just then, the ground shook with the giant's steps, and the good woman's face turned pale. She threw the remnants of Jack's meal into a cupboard. "Hide!" she said, and pushed Jack into a closet, thrusting the bag of golden eggs after him just in time. Jack crouched very still and watched through the keyhole as the giant entered the room.

"Why do you not greet your husband at the door, as a proper wife should?!" shouted the great ogre. Upon the hearthstone he slapped down three slain boars that he carried under his arm as easily as one might hold a basket of kittens. "Make a fire!" he commanded. "I'm hungry."

With considerable effort, his wife hefted the giant's hatchet to her shoulder and started for the door, but the giant stopped her, having spied some crumbs of bread upon the table. He looked about suspiciously. "Who eats bread in this house before midday?" Turning on his wife, he demanded, "Have you entertained a guest?!" His great brows knit together, and he sniffed the air. "Methinks I smell the blood of an Englishman!"

"Why, it...it was only I, husband...I who was eating the bread," stammered the woman, "And what you smell must be these English herbs drying on the stove."

The giant swept the crumbs onto the floor. They landed inches short of the dog, which was making itself small in the corner. The cowering dog stretched its neck to sniff at the crumbs, but did not venture forth, though it was lean and hungry. The giant said to the woman, "You will grow as fat as a hog and reduce me to poverty with such gluttony."

"I am sorry, husband. I had hoped to please you. So often you have complained of my spare figure. Yesterday you called me a walking skeleton. You said it gave you a fright to wake beside me in our bed."

"Fat or thin will make no difference," he said. "Either way, you would give a man a fright." At this, he chortled and pounded his fist upon the table. The woman's eyes filled with tears, which she tried to blink away. From the giant's bullish nostrils there issued a contemptuous snort that fluttered the curtains and unsettled the ashes in the fireplace. "Cover up that wretched face!" he bellowed. "Do you never recognize a joke when you hear it? I am weary of your sulks and fits. Here am I, your husband, returned from having swum an uncharted sea and back again, from traveling the length of a barbarous land where I left the carcasses of its pitiful defenders broken in ditches, and from climbing the sheer face of a heartless, icy mountain," he boasted, "and what do I come home to but *this*!" He gripped her chin between his huge fingers, pushed her toward the mirror, and forced her to contemplate her joyless reflection before releasing her.

Trying to appease him, she exclaimed, "Oh, husband, how do you find the courage to risk such dangers as those you have spoken of?"

"How?" he sneered. "Because I am not a lazy, mewling cat like you, content only to climb a flight of stairs and conquer the dust and spiders of my own attic."

Then he left the room to rest on his bed. Soon all the windows of the house rattled to his monstrous snores. Trembling, the giant's wife ran to the closet and opened the door.

"Go, quickly," she whispered to Jack, "before he wakes!"

But Jack could not bring himself to leave her in such a plight. He begged her to descend the beanstalk with him. "When we reach the bottom, I will chop the beanstalk down so your husband cannot discover it and follow. Then you will never know want or loneliness again. My mother will welcome you as a sister. You shall be treated kindly, instead of threatened and mocked and vexed to tears."

But the giant's wife refused. "It would be wrong of me," she said. "I have already betrayed one husband by allowing you to enter his household after his many warnings about Englishmen. You see that he was right, for I have deprived my second husband of a brother and a fortune." Jack started to speak, but she gently silenced him. "No, young Jack, it was not your fault. You were only a boy doing your duty by your poor widowed mother. I was to blame."

"But good mistress," he blurted, "the giant earned his fate by his cruelty to you."

"Nay, Jack. Surely you do not think that anyone deserves an untimely death. And I would be a poor wife indeed if I could not bear a husband's occasional fits of temper."

Jack could not understand how the giant's wife could view her husband's behavior with such tolerance, and he begged her again to come away. He described how his own father had lived harmoniously with his mother before he died and that the two had daily shown their fondness for one another in small deeds of generosity. "You should expect no less," he asserted. "Leave him and find the happiness you deserve!"

The good woman feared that the giant would soon be wakened by Jack's importunate pleas. "Perhaps you are right, dear boy," she said, to placate him. "My husband should cultivate a more generous spirit, for his own sake at least. I would hate to see the doors of heaven shut to him when someday he tries to enter. I promise I will speak to him about it. If I put it to him as you have done to me, surely he will see reason."

Jack was doubtful and opened his mouth to protest again, but the giant's wife, thinking she heard her husband stirring upstairs, held a finger to Jack's lips. She said in a low voice, "It is not easy for folk to change their nature. Perhaps he will need time to consider. After I speak to him about it, I will wait six months for him to improve his ways. If he does not, then I shall climb down the beanstalk to you and your good mother."

Jack left, and walked back along the road with a heavy heart. When he came to the cloud bog, he waded in until his feet found the sturdy vine. Then he made his arduous way down the beanstalk to his house, where he rested from weariness. He told his mother what had taken place, but all she said was, "Ah," and shook her head sadly.

Thence, for six months, at every dawn, Jack lay in his bed watching the sun's first rays flicker in the broad leaves of the beanstalk outside his window, wondering if the giant's wife would soon climb down and begin a happier life. When half a year had passed, he prayed the good woman's failure to appear meant that the giant had had a change of heart. At the end of the eighth month, Jack could no longer bear the anxiety of not knowing. He made up his mind to climb again and learn the woman's fate.

When, after the perilous ascent to the top of the beanstalk, he emerged from the clouds, he saw the giant's house in the distance once more, but the nearer he drew, the more desolate it appeared. The windows were shut tight and the curtains drawn. Flowers lay brown and wilted near the door. All was silent. Even the birds and crickets seemed subdued. Jack crept to a window and peered through a gap in the curtain. There he saw the kitchen where he had hidden from the giant. In a chair near the cold hearth sat the giant's wife, bent in the shoulders and listless of eye, her hands hanging limp at her sides. The giant strolled about the room, speaking in a harsh, accusing voice. Occasionally he punctuated his speech with a slap of his hand upon the table, causing the crockery to jump and the woman's shoulders to stiffen. She said nothing except when he demanded a reply, which she murmured in words so low that Jack could not hear them.

"You are good for nothing!" the giant was shouting. "If I had not married you, you would have starved and gone to your grave by now. What are you fit for but to plump cushions and set the cups straight on a tea tray?" He stopped pacing and towered over her. "What an odious sight you are. Yet you have the insolence to complain of my behavior and dare threaten to seek happiness elsewhere!" He bared his teeth and gave a harsh, sneering laugh, like the sound of a rusted gate thrust suddenly open. "Do you think others will have more patience than I with a worthless, ungrateful strumpet who abandons her husband?"

Again she murmured something that Jack could not hear, and the giant scowled and shouted into her face, "I'm sick to death of your measly, mincing little voice! Speak up!" The woman's chest rose with an effort to take a breath, and she said in a voice only slightly more distinct, "Please, husband,

I mentioned such ideas so many months go, and only in passing. I know now my thoughts were quite mistaken, as I have told you many times."

"Oh, fine words, indeed! But I know better how treachery festers in such a weak and foolish mind as yours. Like all women, you connive and wait your chance to betray."

Suddenly he slumped back onto his great throne-like chair with a resounding smack, which shivered the window pane where Jack pressed his ear. "What a life!" the giant groaned. He shook his head slowly from side to side. "Out of the goodness of my heart I wed my brother's penniless widow, though she be a puny, whining sort of female. How much happier I would be now if I could have found a strong, plump young maiden of my own size. A goodly armful to share my bed and put food on the table equal to my appetites. You—" he turned to her accusingly, "would make a better wife for a middling-sized flea." Once more Jack saw the woman struggle to keep tears from falling. He had to prevent himself from bursting into the house and confronting the ogre, but he could well imagine how such an impulsive action would end.

Finally, the giant went to his bedchamber to sleep. His wife continued for some minutes to sit in her chair without moving as if there were no spirit left in her. A brace of bloody lambs lay on the hearth stone, skinned and ready for the spit. At last she rose, picked up the giant's heavy hatchet and walked with leaden steps to the woodpile in the yard to chop wood for the fire. Jack followed quietly and watched the woman at her work. Despite her pinched and peaked appearance she wielded the outsized hatchet with more vigor than he thought possible, as if each stroke relieved an inward anger. Then, suddenly, she looked up and saw Jack. At the sight of him, there passed across her own pale face a flush of happiness, followed at once by a look of shame and apprehension.

Jack stepped forward. "Once again it appears I have brought you trouble, good lady," said he. "You are punished for the boldness I urged upon you."

She cast a furtive glance up toward the window where her husband slept, then put down the hatchet and drew Jack to a doorway sheltered from the window's view. "Nay, young Jack," she said in a low tone, "it is my fault alone, for I could not explain it to him as fluently as you did to me. When he glares with that great beetled brow and pounds upon the table, my reason flies away and my tongue ties itself in knots, for I am not a clever woman." She gazed dully at the pile of wood she had yet to chop into kindling. "In any case," she said, taking a deep breath as if to strengthen her resolve, "'tis better after all that I remain here. Though he rues the day he married me, he would be unhappier still if I abandoned him, else why did he rage so when I talked of leaving? Pray, do not concern yourself about me. Things are going better now than before."

"Do you mean that things went worse than *this*?"

"Only for a little while, after I asked him to moderate his temper. Then his fury continued night and day, but now it comes and goes with some measure of peace in between, and of course he leaves to have adventures, as always." She looked off into the yard for a moment and said, musingly, "If I had not expressed myself to him so unsurely, I think I might have convinced him, for he is a fair-minded man—"

"Fair-minded!"

"Knowing I would be unfit to live among ordinary folk, he does not cast me off in spite of my deficiencies. He has so many virtues, while I am lacking in all."

"What virtues has he?!"

"He is a brave man. I have nothing of his courage and resourcefulness. It is no wonder he hates my company. If others..." Her voice trailed off despondently.

Jack searched for an argument that would convince the good woman to come away with him. At last he pleaded with her to accompany him to the beanstalk if only to say goodbye, since her husband was sleeping so soundly. The giant's even snores could be heard through the thick pane of his window two stories high, and the woman admitted that the ogre would sleep for an hour or more. So relenting, she followed Jack down the road to the place where the tip of the beanstalk was hidden. Lifting her skirts, she waded with Jack a little way into the vapors. Then he took her hand and guided it down through the mist until it grasped a thick, curved bean pod as long as his arm.

"Ah!" exclaimed the giant's wife. "I hardly believed you until you showed me! Who would guess this great vine grows from below!" Jack pried the pod partly open and withdrew a brown mottled seed as large as an egg and lobed like a heart. He placed it in her hand and told her how he had grown the new beanstalk from the old one by just such a seed as this. With such conversation, he delayed his descent for as long as possible, still hoping she would change her mind and follow him, but to no avail.

Before they parted, she said, "May I keep this bean to remember you by?"

"You've no need to ask," he replied. "It is yours, and many more besides, if you like."

"No." she said, pensively. Turning the seed in her hand, she seemed to study it. "I need just this one." She tied the bean in her handkerchief, then lent Jack a hand down and he stepped upon the highest branch of the beanstalk as if upon the top rung of a ladder. She thanked him for the seed and waved a farewell. That was the last he saw of her before he descended into the cloud.

Jack returned to his mother and related all he had learned of the woman's circumstances and her determination to remain with the giant who treated her so ill. His mother shook her head. "I'm afraid it is often so with women who do not know their own worth," she said.

ॐ

Some weeks later Jack and his mother woke to a booming clap of thunder that shook their cottage. They ran to a window to look up at the storm, but found the sky blue and clear. Then they thought of the thunderous crash that shook the earth when the first beanstalk had fallen to the ground so many years ago. They hurried outside to see if the beanstalk had toppled, but the gnarled, spiraling vine still soared to its cloud cover just as it had when they went to bed the night before.

"Now that she has made up her mind not to come down to us," Jack's mother gently urged, "you had best chop down the beanstalk before the giant happens to wade into the bog and discover it."

Jack did as his mother requested. But when the prodigious vine fell and its scattered parts covered all the yard, Jack felt much remorse and uneasiness, for now the giant's wife had no route by which to escape the ogre. From this cause, he saved out one last bean and hid it.

ॐ

It was three years before his conscience again got the better of him. Early one morning, while his mother slept, he removed the bean from its hiding place and sowed it in the ground. Another beanstalk grew. Without delay Jack made the strenuous climb to the top.

When he emerged from the vapor, he was amazed to see how much had changed. An arbor, thick with leaves and laden with plump purple grapes, ran along either side of the once barren, dusty road. He hurried toward the house, surprised, as he drew closer, to see it freshly painted and trimmed in gay colors, its doors and windows open to the sunshine. A lively flock of guineas pecked among a profusion of buttercups in the yard. Frocks and petticoats fluttered on the line.

While gazing in wonder at this sight, he was overtaken by a woodcutter's cart clattering toward the house with a load of wood. Jack hailed the driver, a pleasant-featured fellow with the ox-like back and shoulders of men of his trade.

"Is the mistress at home, do you know?" said Jack, tilting his head toward the house.

"Nay," replied the woodcutter. "Likely she's gone to market to buy more chicks and another cow or two. By God's grace she is a prosperous woman."

"How so?" said Jack.

"Haven't you heard? Why, you must come from other parts."

"I do."

"Then, you don't know that once she was a pitiful creature, held captive and ill-treated by her husband, a monstrous ogre. One day, some three years past, an enormous beanstalk miraculously grew in her garden. It blossomed and came to bear in one night, they say. To harvest all its beans, she had to chop it down completely, so tall it was, every pod the size of a scythe blade." The woodcutter shaded his eyes for a moment to look up at a cloud that hung in the sky over the giant's house. "The beanstalk had grown up higher than that cloud, and was as thick and tough as ironwood. But the ogre's wife knew how to wield an axe and was a resourceful woman. After she felled the stalk, she ground the beans and sewed them up in bags to sell to all the farmers hereabouts for feed. They do say that pigs raised on those beans are too big to keep in ordinary pens. With her earnings, she set up in the dairy trade."

"But her husband, the ogre," said Jack, scarcely able to believe what he was hearing, "he allowed his wife such freedom?"

"Nay," said the man. "It is certain he never would have. That is another of God's blessings, for a little after the beanstalk appeared, the ogre vanished. A-roaming, or a-sailing, or a-climbing, everyone thinks. He was of a nature to do such things. Usually he came back in a week or a fortnight to plague the good woman, but this time he never returned at all. He has been gone these three years and seems to be gone for good. Maybe he came afoul of a greater ogre and got the worst of it. No one knows. Some say he'll come back to torment her again, but—good soul that she is—she goes about her business untroubled as if she has not a care in the world."

Jack thanked the man for the information and allowed him to go his way. For some while, he stood and surveyed the thriving domain of the giant's wife. Musing on the unexpected turn of events, he gazed up at the cloud that hung so far above the house, and idly fingered the bean he had brought with him in his pocket to give to the woman who had been so kind to him. Then all at once it occurred to him what had taken place. Hastily, he fastened his pocket tight to keep the bean from accidentally falling on the ground.

Then he turned, after taking one more look at the cloud and the house and the garden, and retraced his steps. When the woodcutter passed by in his cart again on his way back to town, Jack tipped his hat politely and waited until the man was out of sight. Then he walked into the mist and let himself down the beanstalk at a leisurely pace.

THE ONE-ARMED SHEPHERD

A shepherd stood musing on a hillside from which he could survey the length and breadth of his small domain. He looked down upon his little thatched cottage with smoke drifting from its chimney, the kitchen garden where his wife was gathering rosemary to sweeten potatoes for their supper, the copse of willows beneath which two of his children were coaxing a straying ewe lamb back to the fold.

Finally the shepherd gazed down upon the clear winding brook which ran through his land and away into the wilderness. Tracing its wandering twists and turns, he noticed, to his alarm, that upstream, where the brook ran through his wealthy neighbor's property, a swarm of laborers were carting and dropping boulders into the stream. As he watched in astonishment a team of men equipped with ropes dragged great boulders from a field, rolled them down the bank, waded in and pushed them into place. Before the shepherd could comprehend the meaning of this activity, one last great stone was joined with the others and the stream flowed no more.

The shepherd ran down the hill to tell his wife. After anxious discussion they resolved to speak with their neighbor, with whom they had never before had any discourse, for he was far above them in station. At once, they hurried to his house, but it was several hours before they were allowed into his presence. Even then they were required to stand humbly in the doorway of his receiving room, as he was protective of his imported carpets.

"Please sir," said the shepherd. "Your dam has dried up our stream, leaving no water for our sheep. They will die of thirst and our family will starve."

"I have interest in neither your sheep nor your family," said the man, seated comfortably in a capacious armchair. His hands lay folded over a gap in his waistcoat, unbuttoned to accommodate his corpulent belly.

"But the stream is for all to use," protested the shepherd. "That is the law."

The man said, "In that case, talk of it to your neighbors downstream and perhaps they will convince me of a public interest in removing my dam."

In a voice shaking with ire, the shepherd's wife spoke up. "You know full well that the stream meanders into the wilderness and ends on no one's land after ours."

"That is a pity," said the rich man. "But I am in need of a lake, for I am fond of gazing upon swans and water lilies. Neither of these thrives in a moving stream."

The shepherd protested, "When you stop our stream, you take water which is not rightfully yours. It is a criminal act."

"Then I advise you to take your case to court," said the man, with a cruel smile, and dismissed them.

Wife and husband talked far into the night about what to do. Without water, they would lose their little flock and their garden and have to give up the small cottage that the shepherd had worked so hard to build. Such forfeiture would be especially bitter, for the shepherd was a one-armed man, having lost his right arm in his youth. Thus, all work was double for him and all his achievements hard-won.

If they lost their stream and their flock, he and his wife would have to hire out their labor to others, and the labor of their seven children, as well. This pained him most of all because he had always allowed his children to tend the family's sheep in pairs and threes in order to spare them the solitary shepherd's loneliness which he had suffered as a boy.

❧

The shepherd and his wife decided to travel to the magistrate court and present their case. As there was not enough money to hire a lawyer, they had no choice but to plead it themselves. With their youngest child—a babe still at the breast—they traveled all day and far into the night, to the distant provincial court, where, after sleeping wrapped in sheepskins upon the cold ground, they appeared, bearing an old tattered deed to their land. The shepherd's rich neighbor was not in attendance, but was represented by three lawyers, splendid in velvet robes and starched ruffs.

Holding out the deed in his one hand, the shepherd offered the document in evidence to the bewigged and black-frocked magistrates seated above him on their benches. Then he stated his case in a subdued and humble manner. When he had finished, the chief magistrate addressed the three lawyers.

"The complainant accuses the defendant of damaging the value of his property by building a dam." His voice drawled and his eyelids drooped as if he were ready for sleep, though it was but mid-morning. "What evidence does the defendant offer?" One of the lawyers rose and looked down his spectacles at fine, close writing on a long scroll of parchment, from which he then read in a droning voice.

The document claimed that the land downstream of the

contested dam was ancestral land belonging not to the shepherd, but to his neighbor. It had been acquired so long ago that a deed no longer existed. The shepherd—so the lawyer said—had been allowed to use this land by the owner's family, though it rightfully belonged to them.

The shepherd could not believe his ears. He leapt to his feet. "But my deed!" he cried, gesturing with his one arm to the worn and faded paper that lay upon the table.

"Order in the court!" shouted the magistrate so severely that the shepherd's infant asleep on its mother's breast, woke and cried. A bailiff took the shepherdess roughly by the elbow and escorted her with her baby out of the courtroom.

"What have you to say regarding this man's deed?" said the magistrate to the three lawyers. After conferring briefly, the second of the three stood up.

"The shepherd's deed is entirely fraudulent," the lawyer said.

The magistrate examined the much folded and torn document with some fastidiousness, holding it between thumb and forefinger as if it carried a disease. "What evidence have you that the thing is fraudulent?" he asked.

The third lawyer rose to explain. "We have witnesses who are prepared to testify."

"Call them, then," the magistrate replied, and three men—farmers, by the look of their rough clothes and brown, lined faces—were brought into the courtroom, hats in hand. They had come from the province many miles distant where the shepherd had once lived as a youth. The magistrate eyed them blandly. "What have these men to say about the shepherd's deed?"

"They know nothing of the deed," said the lawyer, "only that the shepherd is a liar and deceiver."

The first farmer came forth with the story and the two others attested to its accuracy. "Twice did this shepherd cry, 'Wolf!' for the pleasure of watching us—young laborers then, at the end of a long day's work—scramble in haste up a steep hill to help him."

"'Help! Wolf! Help!' he cried," chimed in the second farmer, "and laughed boldly in our faces to see our alarm, for there *had* been a danger of wolves, but there was no wolf at the time that he called."

The third farmer stepped forward indignantly. "And after we chided him—gently the first time, with much forbearance, and even sharing drink with him—he played the devilish trick a second time! But God punished the villain." The other two farmers nodded complacently.

"Indeed?" said the magistrate. "In what manner?"

"God sent a real wolf—" said the first farmer.

"—who, after devouring a lamb of the shepherd's master," piped up the second, "attacked the shepherd himself. Naturally we did not come to his aid when he cried 'Wolf!' a third time. How could we believe him after he had lied and mocked us twice? His punishment was to lose an arm to the wolf's hungry jaws. God in his mercy did not let the shepherd die, although no one would have been surprised or aggrieved if He had."

The magistrate, turned now to the shepherd for an accounting of himself. "What say you to these accusations?" The shepherd looked about for his wife, whose kind and loving eyes he had relied on to calm him, but she waited helplessly out of sight in the entry hall with her wailing baby. "Did you or did you not cry 'Wolf!' twice for the sport of it?"

The age-old pain in the stump of the shepherd's arm began to throb, and the jaws of the wolf suddenly loomed. He could feel the curved yellow fangs sinking into his flesh. He could hear the rip of his muscles pulling from the bones, the snap of the ligaments separating at his shoulder, the screams that had issued from his own throat. For some minutes as he faced the court he felt dizzy and could not speak, though all eyes were fastened upon him. Words to answer the magistrate's question did not come to him, for he was lost in time, standing friendless and alone on the hillside where he tended the sheep so many years ago.

He was but a boy then—whiskers had not yet grown upon his face—how old in years he did not know. He had been orphaned as a small child and his labor sold to the master who owned the flocks. Below the slopes where the sheep grazed, other lads had worked companionably side-by-side, ploughing, sowing, harvesting, and driving the farmers' stock to the bustling marketplace. They sang and laughed and tussled with each other as they worked, while he sat upon his hillside by himself and longed to be among them.

He remembered the day his master climbed the hill and said these words, "My neighbor's flock is cut in half by a wolf's ravages. I do not want my sheep to go the way of his. Mind you keep a sharp eye out and whistle for help if a wolf comes near." He gave him a willow whistle for that purpose.

The boy kept an eye out as he was told, and at night his sleep was wakeful and his dreams full of yellow-eyed wolves with sharp teeth. During the long, fear-filled days and nights, his loneliness grew keener than ever. Then there came an evening, just as the farmers' lads had finished their toil and were walking home, singing and making merry together, when he raised the whistle to his mouth and, scarcely aware of what he was doing, blew. The lads below looked up to where he stood alone on the hilltop. He cried, "Wolf! Help! Wolf!" And the lads, brandishing their hoes and threshing tools, came running up the hill to his aid.

When they arrived, panting and sweating, and saw no sign of a wolf anywhere from there to the horizon, they asked, perplexed, "Where is it?" He laughed with nervousness and shame and admitted it was only a joke after all. The boys shook their heads in disgust and upbraided him for mocking them. They called him a knave and the son of a dog and other insulting names. But the golden sun was just then setting on the far horizon, and the view of the valley in the gathering mist was so beautiful that the lads, who seldom raised their eyes above their ploughs, said, "Well, well, now that we are here, let us sit a moment and rest from our labors." And they sat and admired the view and accepted the shepherd's apologies. Their hurried climb had made them thirsty, so they took out wine sacks and drank from them, good-naturedly offering drafts to him. He drank and sat next to the lads in the grass, leaning back on his elbows just as they did, until the stars came out and they said good-bye and descended the hill to their homes. He remembered now how he lay in the darkness for many hours afterwards, more content than he had ever been in his life.

The next evening he looked down again at the lads leaving their fields and walking along the road at the end of the day. He thought of the lonely night ahead of him and the wakeful vigil he must keep. As if moved by another's will, his fingers found the whistle in his pocket and brought it to his lips again. The lads looked up toward the sound and heard his urgent call, "Help! Wolf! Help!" He saw them turn to each other in consternation.

Perhaps they could not imagine that he would be so brash as

to trick them again. They rushed to the top of the hill. "Where is the wolf?" they shouted, and he stammered and laughed nervously, knowing how feeble his lie would sound. He told them the wolf ran off when it heard them coming. The lads looked in every direction, but could see only sheep from there to the horizon. "No wolf alive can run so swiftly as that!" they asserted, and this time they cuffed him and shoved him to the ground and shook their fists at him, threatening worse if he ever tried the trick again. He lay that night alone under the stars and could not hold back tears, knowing he had done wrong and now had lost all hope of companionship.

The next day he tended his sheep dolefully, too listless to follow the strays into the hollows and bring them back to the safety of the flock. As the sun began to set, he dreaded the coming night. Then he heard from far away the shrill bleating of a lamb in distress and leaped up to follow the sound. When he found the lamb it was caught in the jaws of a great and grizzled wolf. A ewe, the lamb's mother, cried in helpless anguish nearby. His heart beating wildly, he picked up a stick and brandished it at the wolf, but the wolf only turned its gaze upon him as if to say, "I will eat you next."

ک

Now, standing confronted in the magistrates' court, the shepherd remembered his frantic haste as he ran stumbling to the top of the hill and blew and blew on his willow whistle.

ک

"Help! Wolf! Help!" he had screamed, in a voice choking with terror. "The wolf has caught my master's lamb! Help! Oh, please! Help!" The homeward-bound lads looked up, but only laughed. One shouted in a loud, derisive voice, "Liar!

Only fools would be taken in a third time!" And they shook their scythes at him and kept on their way.

He shivered as dark descended. The slain lamb's pitiful bleating was silenced but the ewe continued to mourn. As the moon rose, the shepherd listened and watched. When the wolf climbed the rise of the hill and pounced upon him, he could do nothing to defend himself. If its belly had not been full of the succulent lamb, the wolf would have eaten him from head to toe, but the beast was content with a morsel. The slavering creature tore off the shepherd's right arm and loped away with it into the night, leaving him for dead.

For two days he lay at death's door until his master climbed the hill to bid him bring the sheep down for shearing. When the news of his condition reached the village, many said it served him right. The lads had spread word of his tricks and there was little sympathy for him. His master discharged him from his job, leaving him starving and without shelter as he lay close to death.

Then a miracle took place. A young shepherdess who herded her parents' small flocks near a neighboring village took pity on him. He had awakened from a feverish delirium to the touch of a cool hand on his brow and the sight of sweet brown eyes in a plain honest face gazing tenderly at him. Instead of rocky earth and a cruel night wind for a bed and blanket, he found himself lying on fragrant straw and covered by a fleece.

The shepherdess came every day and nursed him to health, feeding him, cleaning his wounds, and talking of her own loneliness among her flocks. He thought of his joy when she grew to love him, one-armed and weak though he was, and how they married and left the unforgiving province of their birth, and saved a bit of money and bought two thin, sickly lambs, which lived and flourished.

It seemed that good fortune had smiled upon him at last. The lambs produced more lambs until there was a little flock, and he and his wife began to have offspring of their own. After years of incessant toil and thrift, they had a winter shelter for their sheep and a tiny cottage for their family. Flowering vines wreathed the doorway where their children played. A garden supplied their needs. The pretty stream kept it watered, and watered the sheep as well. The family grew as the years passed, and though the shepherd and his wife made but a meager living and their work was hard indeed, especially his—accomplished one-armed—they were happier than they thought possible, their former loneliness dispelled.

ॐ

All these things the shepherd remembered and longed to express, as he stood before the magistrates, trying to put his thoughts into words. At last, he said, "My Lords, I...I..."

"Did you or did you not falsely cry 'Wolf!'?" the lawyer broke in. The shepherd's mouth closed, then opened again, but the words he intended to speak would not come out. "It is clear," said the lawyer to the magistrates, "that even now he is fabricating a lie."

The chief magistrate said, "Answer the question, as you were told to."

"Yes," said the shepherd, "I did cry 'Wolf!' once—"

"Only once? Not twice?" said the lawyer.

"Twice, sir, but—"

"You see, My Lords, how he tries to minimize his guilt?"

"By '*once,*' " the shepherd, struggled to say, "I only meant '*then, at that time,*' for I was not a man then, but a boy—"

"A boy? Of what age were you?"

"I do not know exactly. You see—"

The lawyer sneered, "The man does not know his own age exactly?"

The first lawyer stood again. "If you are not a liar," said he, "have you witnesses who will attest to your character?"

"My wife—" said the shepherd.

The magistrate interrupted. "A wife may not testify for a husband."

"Except for your wife," pressed the lawyer, "you have no one who will speak up for your honesty?"

The shepherd stared at the three lawyers with their raised eyebrows and supercilious eyes looking down at him through pinching spectacles, their quills held poised to scribble any incriminating word he might utter in confusion. He glanced at the pale, smooth hands—unroughened by labor—that held the quills. Suddenly his face turned livid.

He shouted, "Who *should* I get to speak for me? The folk who know me well? All are poor, as I am! How can they spare three days from their labors to travel to court? With what riches do you expect me to pay their costs? My wife and I, with our nursing child, did well to find a patch of dry ground to sleep on, coming here!" The chief magistrate pounded his gavel and shouted for order, but the shepherd was too angry to be silenced. "My rich neighbor compensates these farmers well for their journey and lost work! He pays lawyers and hirelings good money to hunt down my past and throw it in my face!"

The third lawyer rose to protest, "This disrespectful outburst is evidence of the man's arrogance and incivility!" The magistrate mildly bade the lawyer be seated. In a tone of jaded curiosity, he asked the shepherd, "What came over you to cry "Wolf!" the second time? Anyone with sense, even a liar, could have anticipated a beating."

"Unless he is both a liar and a simpleton!" said the lawyer. The magistrate ignored the comment.

The shepherd's face grew red again, but from shame. He remembered what had come over him those many years ago.

Eyes fixed on the floor, he murmured, "I was lonely, you see—"

A collective snort issued from the lawyers' side of the bench.

The magistrate squinted down at the shepherd as if he were an exotic insect.

"'Lonely,' you say! Do you mean to tell us that with only the excuse of loneliness you tricked hardworking men into coming selflessly to your rescue and forfeiting a deserved rest from their day's labors?"

"They were not men, but boys, too. We were all boys, you see. Boys...and...and...I didn't mean them any harm."

"No *harm*? Then what *did* you mean?" demanded the first lawyer, rising again.

"I don't know. I don't know," said the shepherd. "But I am not a liar...any more." He pointed to the deed on the magistrate's table. "It is authentic. It was signed in this very court. See the signatures." The magistrates peered down at the deed and conferred with each other in low tones. The chief magistrate wrote some words upon a sheet of parchment. The others, with nods and murmurs, seemed to concur with what he wrote.

At last the magistrate told the shepherd, "The signatures on your document are blurred and unreadable, perhaps made so deliberately. In any case none of us remembers signing it."

"*I* remember," said the shepherd, desperately, "but..." he faltered, "...perhaps I am mistaken. It was many years ago. Maybe *other* magistrates—" The pounding of the gavel cut him off.

"Enough!" declared the chief magistrate. He stood. With a gesture, he brought the lawyers to their feet as well. Ceremoniously, he read the opinion that he had written: "This court, in consideration of the complainant's attested character as a liar and in consideration of his inability to prove the authenticity of his deed, finds in favor of the defendant. The land belongs to him and him alone. As there are no legal landholders below the stream, there can be no objection to his damming it."

᠙

For presenting a false document, the shepherd was fined three gold pieces. For perjury, two. He was able to pay the fines only by selling his little flock and the furnishings—such as they were—of his cottage, from which he was soon evicted. He, with his wife and infant, roamed from farm to farm in search of work. The older children scattered, one by one, through the province to find employment in the only trade they knew. Separately and in solitude, they wandered the hills and valleys of their masters' lands in search of lost and straying sheep, but none of the shepherd's children was ever heard falsely to cry "Wolf!"

TO GRANDMOTHER'S HOUSE

The child arrived at the fork in the path and stopped, undecided which way to go. The familiar path to the right would take her to Grandmother's house. The one to the left descended into a deep ravine. From above she could spy the glint of white mushrooms and ferns like ladies' fans. A lattice of twisted roots made a staircase down the steep slope. At the bottom, the path hid itself before emerging from the ferns and disappearing around a bend. What that bend concealed she could discover only by following the path. This she had never done.

She stood there for some time, shifting her heavy basket from hand to hand, when she was startled by an insistent call. *Witchy, witchy, witchy.* Perched on an overhanging branch, a bird, adorned in just such a red cape and peaked hood as her own, cocked its head and gazed at her in a knowing sort of way. Then it spread its scarlet wings, flew to the bottom of the ravine and landed on a gooseberry bush, looking back as if to say, *Why linger? Come down!*

Hesitating only a moment, the child set her basket on the path, scrambled down the root staircase, and in short order was at the very bottom of the ravine. But the redbird had already taken flight again, so the child hastened after it, running as fast as her little legs would carry her. In a moment she was around the bend in the path, under a canopy of oaks that formed a vaulted tunnel striped across by sunlight and shadow. Here the path widened and straightened. The bird flew on ahead, swooping under the arching branches, and oh! how the little girl ran after it! Her feet barely touched the ground and her red cape flew out behind her as if she, too, had wings.

Alas, the bird outraced her and disappeared among the trees. But now the child had a moment to stop and notice her surroundings. The forest was still, except for the drawn-out *shhhhh* of rustling leaves overhead. She wondered if the great oaks had been having a private conversation just before she came into view. One old tree with a twisted trunk leaned into the path, like her grandmother leaning on her cottage gate, the wind wrapping the skirt around her legs. The girl thought, *I must turn back, for Grandmother is expecting me and will be angry if I am late.* But she walked a little farther because the path was taking another turn and looked so inviting. *I will first just see what is around this next bend,* she said.

The path twisted and turned, rose and fell, and every time she was determined to go back, her eye was caught by one thing or another, and she had to hurry forth to examine it.

First, she spied a tree whose lower limb curved out from the trunk and up and in again just like the handle of a mug. She laughed to see such a marvel and ran over to climb up and sit upon it. *I am a tiny elf,* said she, looking down at the ground from the low branch of the silvery-leaved cottonwood. *I am so small I can sit upon the handle of Grandmother's mug, and she does not even see me.* The branches hung down like the old woman's silver tresses. *And now Grandmother will lift her mug and drink some wine!* And the little girl hopped off in time to avoid being squeezed by her grandmother's gnarled fingers.

Next, she came upon a thick-bodied snake sunning itself

across the middle of the path. The snake had a band of brown arrows all down its back and rows of spots along its sides. When she approached, though she walked on tiptoe, it opened its lazy eyes and slid itself into a coil as tight as her mother's braid after she had wound it in a bun and fastened it with pins. The snake stuck its tongue out several times in succession. She tried to return the greeting but could not do it half so well, for her own tongue was slow and would not fork. To avoid disturbing the snake, the child stepped into the brush, walked around it and continued on her way.

Farther along, she spied a squirrel blackening its mouth on a walnut. The creature scurried up a tree when it saw her coming, and she picked up the discarded walnut shell and rubbed her hands on the half-eaten husk, for she knew it would give her skin a lovely lemony smell, and indeed, when she held her hands to her nose, they were perfumed. Continuing down the path, she found more walnuts, scattered here and there. At each one she freshened her perfume, and before long her hands were as black as the squirrel's mouth.

I must find a stream to wash in, she thought, *or Grandmother will scold*. No sooner had she expressed this wish than she came upon a lively brook crossing the path beyond the next turning. She ran up to kneel beside it and washed her hands until they were quite clean. As she washed, little fishes swam past, rippling the reflection of her face, and when she thrust her hands again into the cool water, more fishes glided between her spread fingers. She wondered what they thought, seeing the ten pale fingers, bent at an odd angle by the watery light. Perhaps they commented to each other as they swam past, *How came these stiles to be here when there were none yesterday? I do hope they don't expect us to pay a penny to pass through!*

She was hot after her long walk and took off her red hooded

cape and hung it on a brave little willow that grew right out of the stream from a crevice between two rocks. Though she was often admonished by her mother not to go about shoeless, she could not resist unlacing her boots and leaving them on the bank of the brook while she waded in.

The soles of her bare feet fit snugly around the curves of mossy rocks. Green lichen oozed between her toes and the clear water rippled and swirled around her ankles. Beyond the rocks, the footing turned to smooth, soft sand, so she waded downstream a ways, stopping to smack a bare foot upon the shallow water with a smart splash. For a good while then, she stamped and splashed and stamped and splashed, making a wonderful noise.

When she tired of this game, she waded to her waist into a part of the stream where rocks and fallen logs had made a pool edged with reeds. Here, she watched the widening circles that appeared each time an insect lit upon the surface. She hoped to wear a water circlet for a belt, but each time she approached one, it lost its shape. Now she laced her fingers tightly and dipped them into the pool. When she lifted them out, water floated in the skin bowl of her hands. She drank from it and plunged her hands in for more. Having drunk her fill, she dipped for water again and poured it over her head, sending water fairies tumbling down her forehead, into her eyebrows, down her nose and cheeks until they jumped back into the stream, *drip drop drip*, where they melted away.

By the time she waded back along the stream, up the bank, and onto the path, her skirts were sopping and her sleeves soaked from frill to elbow. Oh, what would her grandmother say to see her in such a state! *You will leave puddles on my good wool carpet, child!* The little girl wrung out her clothes as well as she could, but still they dripped. She thought it best to carry on down the path just a ways farther so that her clothes might dry, and then it would be safe to turn back. For some while, as she continued on her way, the water pattered onto the dead leaves, *drip, drop, drip,* and she marched along briskly in time to it. Drip, drop, drip, then more slowly, *drip . . drop . .* and slower still until she waited a very long time for another drip, but it didn't come because the sun had completely dried her clothes.

Where had the sun come from? It dazzled her eyes. The overarching trees were behind her now, for the path had emerged from the forest to skirt a secret meadow dense with wildflowers. Pink and yellow blossoms littered the path like confetti as if a parade had gone by. Bordering the meadow, a thick patch of raspberry bushes drooped under its load of fruit. To relieve the bushes of their burden and because she was very hungry, the child picked as many berries as she could reach. She sought them even among the thorns, and ate and ate until she was satisfied. Then she filled both apron pockets with berries, one for Grandmother and the other for Mother. When she finished, her arms were crisscrossed with scratches and her pockets were stained bright purple, but she was well-pleased.

Now she glanced about. In the middle of the path, looking for all the world as if eggs had hatched from the ground, twelve white toadstools formed a fairy ring. She ran up to inspect them and found them to be smooth and rounded like velvet cushions. *Perhaps*, thought she, *they are stools for a meeting of the toads.* And as there were no toads sitting on them at the moment, she took the liberty of testing the biggest stool for comfort. Alas, it collapsed under her weight and was crushed beneath her. *I hope that only eleven toads will come to the meeting,* she said, for she did not know where she could find an extra stool for the one she had broken.

Forging her way deeper into the meadow, she was soon up to her shoulders in white daisies, pink gayfeather, yellow goldenrod and purple clover. Sunlight bathed the flowers, and the air was aflutter with butterflies and fur-coated bumblebees bouncing from bloom to bloom. Several times she had to blink a butterfly from her eyelashes, so thickly did they swarm around her. A bumblebee lit upon one of her golden plaits. *"Bzzzz,"* she greeted it, and said again by way of conversation, *"Bzzzz."* The bee lifted off from her hair and, hovering by her face for some moments, replied politely, *"Bzzzz"* before flitting away. Just then, from the corner of her eye she caught sight of something moving in the distance along the path from whence she had come. It was a man.

He carried a longbow and a knife sheathed at his belt and was dressed in the green cap and doublet of a huntsman. The man emerged from the wood stealthily, gazing across the meadow and holding the shaft of an arrow across his great bow as if ready at any moment to let the arrow fly. Just in time, the child ducked down in the grass to hide. If the man should see her, he was certain to say, *Why are you not at your grandmother's house, child? She will be waiting for you. You are naughty to be dawdling so.* But the little girl did not want to return yet, now that she had discovered the secret meadow.

The grasses said *swish swish* as the huntsman pushed slowly through them some distance away, then nearer and nearer, almost coming upon her, then farther away again. While she waited for him to pass by, she sat cross-legged within her screen of flowers, and picked daisies, twisting them into bracelets. Before long, the sun and the buzz of insects made her drowsy. She lay down on her curtained bed of grass, and, even when she could hear the huntsman no more, continued to lie there, looking up into the blue oval of sky. The smells of warm earth and flowers filled her nose. A spotted beetle close to her face made the tiniest of scratching sounds trying to climb a long stem of goldenrod. The last thing the child did before falling asleep was to help the little creature reach the summit of the seedhead.

꒳

A shadow moved across her skin and woke her. Drowsily, she opened her eyes to see a great, tawny dog's face thrust through the curtain of grass and staring in at her. It was just touching her arm with the broad tip of its black nose. She kept her mouth shut tight and watched through the lashes of half-closed lids. The intruder's black-rimmed eyes glowed golden yellow like the agate eyes of her tabby cat. It exhaled hot breath on her skin as it sniffed her up and down. The whiskers that sprouted from its muzzle tickled, but the little girl kept perfectly still and held her breath.

The animal's jaws gaped open now to reveal a long drooling tongue, four curved fangs, up and down, and four rows of sharp incisors. Then, slowly, the pink tongue curled backward along the avenue of teeth. The creature raised its muzzle in the air and closed its eyes for a drawn-out yawn. At this opportunity, the child turned ever so slightly, that she might see the animal better. Its ears, laid back for the yawn, were lined with thick fur. One long, gangly leg was planted inside her nest of grass. On its paw, four lean toes dug their black claws deep in the earth.

The creature, having completed its yawn, glanced at the child, and seeing her changed position, cautiously backed a step away. From this vantage point, it extended only its muzzle to sniff the sole of her bare foot, but at the touch of the wet nose, the little girl could not help jerking the foot back. In an instant, the animal was gone, bounding through the meadow with a hiss of grass that grew fainter as the beast retreated. By the time the child had scrambled to her feet and stood shading her eyes to look after it, it was trotting swiftly along the path at the edge of the forest, its bushy tail held straight out behind.

"Come back," called the child. "Come back! I will not hurt you!" The creature glanced over its shoulder at her once before hastening away. The last she saw of it was the white tip of its dusky tail as the beast slipped silently into the woods. Hastily, she pushed through the tall grasses and struggled up the rise and onto the path, where she called to the animal again and yet a third time, but it did not reappear.

All was quiet. The only sound to be heard was the hollow echo of a woodpecker tapping at a dead tree somewhere deep in the forest. Long shadows were slanting across the path. *I must hurry back now or it will be too late to visit Grandmother and be home before dark.* "When night falls," her mother had warned her, "wolves hunt."

Now she hurried along the path on her bare feet, back the way she had come, stumbling on roots and fallen branches. When she came again to the brook, she lifted her skirts to wade across. In the waning sunlight, she shivered at the cold water swirling around her ankles. She found her boots on the other side and put them on, but the laces were stiff from lying in the mud, and she left them untied.

Her little red hood was no longer draped over the willow tree where she had left it and was nowhere to be seen. *Oh! What will Mother say if I've lost it!* she cried, for her mother had made the beautiful velvet cape with her own hands. The child searched for it along the banks of the brook some distance into the forest, hoping to find it caught up among the reeds and cattails downstream, and at last she was rewarded with a patch of red peeking through the weeds at the edge of the brook. There was the beautiful cape—but it was soiled and covered in cockleburs. *Naughty elves have stolen my cape and made merry pretending to be me, and now it is all dirty!* She picked it up and carried it in her arms, hugging it to herself against the breeze that was bringing gooseflesh up on her skin.

Rustlings and the snapping of twigs told of little animals coming out to eat their suppers now that twilight was near. For a moment she thought that she caught a glimpse of a grayish form, a great, golden-eyed dog, moving through the trees. She hoped it was her shy companion from the meadow, come to accompany her home, but when she stopped to look, it was gone.

Anxious now at the lateness of the hour—*What will Mother say?*—she put her foot upon the path once more and scurried on. She ran so fast that she did not notice the long, arrow-backed creature stretched across the trail until she stumbled over it and fell flat on her stomach, dropping her riding hood in the dirt. Quickly, she got to her feet and looked down to see what had tripped her up. It was the fat, lazy snake who had stuck its tongue out at her. Now the tongue was thrust out of the mouth, the eyes wide and staring in a head that had been freshly chopped off. The body was slit from end to end, cleanly, as if by a sharp knife, the entrails spilling from its belly.

She gasped, shocked to see the snake so still and dead, and sorry for it, too. Bending over it, she touched the strangely dry skin and passed a finger along the jagged pattern on its back. *Good-bye!* she said *Your soul is in Heaven now.* But suddenly she jerked away. The snake's skin under her hand had moved, and she stumbled backward, staring. From the snake's stomach a tiny mouse poked out its nose, then its whole body. The mouse dragged itself out of the snake's entrails to stand motionless on the path. Its fur was matted and stained with filth, its tail and ears bedraggled. It stood dazed for some seconds in the dirt and leaves. Then it stirred, gathered strength, and limped past the child and into the weeds bordering the path.

The little girl straightened and gazed in wonder at the place where the mouse disappeared, and then back at the snake's gutted belly, to wait some minutes for more little creatures to come out. But none did, and she dared not linger, for it was becoming almost too dark to see. She picked up her red cape and ran and ran, passing the tree shaped like a wine mug, running around one bend after another, up one slope and down the next until at last she arrived at the foot of the root staircase that she had first descended. It seemed a steeper and more laborious climb than before, now that she was tired and carrying her cape over one arm, trying to see in the darkness, her bootlaces trailing. Hand over hand, losing her grip and slipping back many times, she finally reached the top of the ravine at the fork in the path where she had set down her basket.

The basket was not where she had left it but lying on its side among the weeds. Its clasp was torn off and only crumbs were left of the cakes. The wine bottle was broken in pieces where it had fallen and shattered against a rock, its contents staining the rock red and soaking into the earth. A mass of tiny handprints facing in many directions were pressed into the damp ground around the basket and leading into the forest. *Goblins have stolen Grandmother's cakes and spilled her wine!* thought the child, in anguish. What shall I do? She stood looking first toward the path to Grandmother's house and then toward the path to home. It is so dark, and I have nothing to bring Grandmother. She will be angry if I don't visit her, but Mother will be angrier at this late hour if I do. After some moments of indecision, she picked up the empty, broken basket and continued along the path toward home.

Unable to see the way clearly as night gathered around her, she walked slowly, blundering often into the brush and having to retrace her faltering steps. She traveled in this erratic manner for some distance when suddenly a long, drawn-out call met her ears, *Woooo woooo woooo*, like the cry of a dog who has seen the full moon. The little girl's heart pounded. She had never seen a wolf, but her mother had told her once when they heard the same cry from far away in the forest, *That is the sound that wolves make when they hunt.* Now the child froze, not knowing whether to hide or run. The sound was moving closer. It seemed to come from just around the next bend. Twigs cracked underfoot and there was a rustle of branches. She held the basket tightly against her chest and stared at the darkness. Amber light flickered through the trees. *The wolf's eyes!* she thought, and shuddered.

Helloooo!…Helloooo!…Helloooo! the voice called, loudly now, and her mother in her familiar gray cloak hurried around the bend, raising a lantern.

"Mother! Mother!" cried the child. "I am here!" and ran straight into her arms.

Her mother dropped to her knees, setting the lantern on the path. "Oh you wicked child! Where have you been?!" She clutched the little girl around the waist. "You frightened me to death!" And after she held the child against her bosom and sobbed out her relief, she stood up without a word and pulled the girl, still clinging to her basket and cape, along the path to home.

حب

As the two entered the yard through the gate, the white cottonball tails of a dozen rabbits bounced away in the darkness while fireflies glittered in the air. The child halted in her tracks at the sight. *The rabbits are stirring up sparks!* she thought. But her mother gave her arm a yank and dragged her along the stone walk and through the door.

Once they were safe inside, her mother glared down at her with eyes widened and brows furrowed in anger. "Look at you!" she shouted. "You have ruined my best basket and torn and stained your clothes and muddied your boots! You are scratched from head to toe and covered in filth. I told you to come home well before nightfall, but you have disobeyed me once again and vexed me and worried me to distraction! How can you treat your mother so?" She shook the child by her little shoulders. "You have done a stupid, foolish thing! You could have been killed by a wolf! You are a terrible, naughty girl and must be punished." The child quaked under this unaccustomed tongue-lashing and went pale with shame and fear. Her mother's mouth was so fierce, pouring out the harsh words and opening and closing to reveal white teeth gleaming in the lantern's light. "No matter what I tell you to do," railed her mother, "it is always the same. You dawdle and idle away the time. And so you have again, haven't you?" The child looked away from her mother's large accusing eyes and could only move her lips in a whisper.

"Speak up, child!" her mother demanded. "I do not have such big ears that I can hear so low a voice. Account for yourself this minute! What happened to you?" She gave the child's shoulders another angry shake.

The little girl suddenly found her voice, though it trembled and broke, and she blurted out her story. "I went to Grandmother's," she exclaimed, "but I met a wolf and he asked where I was going and I told him to Grandmother's so he ran ahead and knocked on Grandmother's door and she thought it was I and let him in, but…and…he ate her up! And then he put on her clothes and then I came and he said 'Come in, Little Red Riding Hood' and I…went in but I thought he couldn't be Grandmother so I said what big eyes you have Grandmother and he said the better to see you with and I said what big ears you have and he said the better to hear you with and I said what a…big mouth you have and he said the better to eat you with—" She stopped to take a breath. Then, with eyes round with horror, she cried, "And he gobbled me up too and we were inside the wolf and the wolf spoiled the basket and ate all the cakes and broke the bottle. But a huntsman came in a green cap and cut the wolf's head off and cut open his belly with his knife and we jumped out and I ran home as fast as I could but then it was after nightfall and I am sorry I could not come home sooner!" Upon these words, she burst into sobs and buried her head in her mother's apron. Heaving a sigh of resignation and shaking her head from side to side, the mother suffered her daughter's tears without further re-monstrance. And with no little mirth, she could not forbear, upon the next market day, to repeat the child's outlandish tale to everyone she met.

THE MILLER'S DAUGHTER

The King gaped at the room that had been filled to the rafters with straw. He gaped at the fifty gold-threaded bobbins stacked in tidy rows on an empty floor glittering with gold dust. Most of all, he gaped at Elsa, the miller's daughter, who sat in a corner by the spinning wheel. Barefoot and clothed in a humble sackcloth dress dyed a deep blue that matched her eyes, she was quite beautiful. Then, too, thought the king, if the royal coffers were ever to dwindle, she could easily replenish them by her talent of spinning gold from straw. Though he had been ready to condemn her to death had she failed at her task, the King now declared she would be his wife.

Much against her will, Elsa was duly crowned and brought to live in the palace. For many months afterwards, she feared that she would be required once more to fulfill her father's rash boast that she could spin straw into gold. She prayed never to have to call on the strange little gnome who had helped her perform this feat, for she did not want him to remember the dreadful promise he had exacted from her. But fortune smiled upon the King's realm: much booty and land were gained in the successful resolution of a war with a rival kingdom, and a great bounty of crops was harvested due to many seasons of clement weather. Her husband was in no need of gold thread.

The early advent of a child capped the King's indifference to Elsa's talent for spinning straw into gold. Indeed, the expectation of a child so pleased him that he promised he would never ask Elsa to make gold again. Spinning of any kind, he declared now, was a lowly task and an unsuitable occupation for a monarch's wife.

When a plump and healthy daughter was born, the King was much pleased and showered the babe with affection. He took the happy event as evidence of the Queen's fertility and the promise of sons and daughters to come. Petting and pampering both his daughter and his wife, he bedecked them in jewels and furs.

Queen Elsa thought perhaps her ordeal was over. Not only had she become rich and brought her parents a comfortable living, but her husband now cherished her, and likewise their daughter. She began to love the King, who, earlier, she had regarded as tyrannical and greedy. Their pleasure in each other blossomed.

Elsa taught the King to appreciate the pastoral sights of a well-thatched roof and the lavender smoke that curled from chimneys amply served by tidy woodpiles. She introduced him to the robust flavor of the bread that made up a peasant's staple fare—hearty loaves made from whole and unrefined rye grain.

For his part, he relished the sighs he could draw from his peasant bride as he wrapped the two of them in satin bedclothes and sank with her into the feather mattress of the royal bed, soft as a cloud. When she was carrying their unborn daughter, he relieved the cravings of her condition with delicacies she had never heard of from foreign lands: quail's eggs, sea oysters, and—her favorite—pomegranates.

When their daughter Pearl was a year old, the strange, gnome-like little man suddenly appeared in Queen Elsa's sitting room to exact his price for the favor he had done her. "Now that the straw is spun to gold," said he, "it is time for you to give me your first-born child."

Elsa turned deadly pale. "Oh no, please! Have mercy!" she beseeched him. "I could not bear to give up my darling girl!"

Moved by the pleasure of prolonging this exercise of his power, the little man promised to release Elsa from her part of the bargain on the condition that she guess his name within three days. Then he skipped gleefully away on his bowed legs, confident that she would never be able to do it.

When he left, Elsa wrung her hands and paced the room. If she could only ask her husband to aid her, he could put the resources of the kingdom at their disposal and quickly discover the strange man's name. But if she told the King the facts, he would know that she had married him under false pretenses and might banish her, or worse.

Still, Elsa was no longer a mere miller's daughter. She was a queen now, with riches of her own. Accordingly, she hired spies and couriers and sent them across the land to discover the creature's name, pledging them to secrecy. By chance, one of them overheard the gnome reciting a self-congratulatory rhyme in which he boasted of his name—even spelling it aloud—and of the impossibility of anyone else's guessing it. The courier reported back to the Queen, who was able to dispatch the little man when he returned, by declaring correctly that his name was Rumpelstiltskin.

At last, Elsa could enjoy her life at court, free to live amenably with her husband the King, and raise her beloved child in peace.

Every month, Elsa took herself away from her royal duties to pay a call on her parents at the mill so they could see their granddaughter, the princess. The child delighted in watching the great millwheel go round. She played happily with children of farmers who brought in their grain. Raising her little velvet skirts and silk petticoats, Pearl hopped with the peasant urchins back and forth over smooth rocks in the mill creek and merrily splashed and was splashed in return.

Elsa urged her parents to visit and dine at the palace, for she loved and missed them, as did the child. But they demurred, pointing out the unseemliness of a miller and his wife appearing at the royal court. After all, they reminded her, Elsa's husband the King had never himself proffered an invitation to them, much as he knew their daughter longed for them to be invited.

As time went by, Elsa came to understand that her parents would not be welcome at the palace and, should she insist on their coming, would be made to feel their lowly station. Indeed, the King had lately begun to correct Elsa herself—his own wife—on such things as diction and table manners.

At first his fault-finding merely annoyed her, but when it persisted, she took grave offense at being thus condescended to. The King appeared to cringe each time the Queen opened her mouth to speak. Her consonants, he declared, were "suety," the way one spoke when one's mouth was full of well-fattened pheasant. And her vowels! Well…! His irritation overcame his restraint when she drew out an *a* as if it were the precursor to a sneeze. At such times he could not resist admonishing her.

She did not take kindly to his correction, and couched her retorts in the clipped and pursey syllables with which *he* habitually spoke, as if a clothespin pinched his nose. She began to imitate his speech to her parents, and he mocked hers to his.

At court, jests and stories were told concerning peasant ignorance and the cupidity of tradespeople. Elsa felt no mirth in hearing these anecdotes, though no one but she found them impolite. For a while she held her tongue, bitterly wishing to contradict the moral of the stories. Indeed, when she thought of the insularity, wastefulness and insipid preoccupations of people at court, she found herself muttering under her breath, "Look who calls the kettle black."

The quantity of crystal, plate and cutlery at every meal appalled her. Why use a spoon for soup? Couldn't one conveniently tip a bowl to drink from it? And was it not sufficient to be provided with a single knife and fork? Yet every place was set with two or three each of different-sized implements, all gold plated, and goblets tall and short for separate wines.

Furthermore, she noticed that people at court did not share. If a nobleman received a boon from the King, he lorded it over the rest. If a noblewoman received a gift of brocade sufficient in length for three gowns, she had all three gowns made for herself alone. Upon being required to choose between the purchase of an emerald tiara and a ruby one, the ladies of the court deplored the necessity of making the choice. They leant upon each others' shoulders in attitudes of woe and, without irony, commiserated over their poverty. Elsa felt the gall rising in her throat at such scenes and had to leave the women's company.

She was made to feel conspicuous for excusing her maids from sleeping on the floor by her bed all night in case she should need to use the chamber pot. "Surely," she said, "I am able to pick up a simple piece of crockery and place it under my own rump!" The King's mother chastised her severely for using the word *rump* in company. "An ox has a rump," she rebuked her. "A lady has a bottom."

Elsa was especially disturbed by jokes about the peasant class's supposed insobriety and general wantonness. Her own parents had been too poor to grow accustomed to strong drink and too worn from work to have much amorous inclination toward one another. Much less did they have the time or energy to dally with and sully the reputations of other peoples' spouses.

Not so abstemious was the aristocracy. Every evening at supper, red-faced, besotted dukes and duchesses not wedded to each other pinched and fondled beneath the tablecloth and knocked their glasses over with inebriated gestures. Such behavior would have so shocked her mother and father that Elsa did not tell them of it

But Elsa had another sorrow, which grew heavier by the month. No more children came after the Princess Pearl. No little brothers or sisters to keep the child company or fulfill the King's wish for a large family and a male heir to his throne.

When Elsa overheard two drunken noblemen bantering about this sad circumstance, her sorrow turned to rage. "These commoners breed like rabbits," said one earl to the other. "If the King had to have chosen a peasant wife, 'tis a pity he had the bad luck to choose a sterile one." "Yes," replied the other. "Undoubtedly, His Majesty expected a good-sized litter from his rabbit."

ॐ

"I refuse to live another day in that household!" Elsa declared to her parents, on a visit home.

"But we gave our word!" cried her father, alarmed.

"*Our* word?"

"Did *you* not say 'I do'?"

"What choice had I, with my own father standing up against me, and all the court in royal attire filling the cathedral to the galleries to ogle the lowly commoner being given away to the King?" She shook her head, aggrieved. "What will happen when my daughter is grown? In such an environment, will not my own child soon learn to scorn me?"

But she forgave her father. Well she knew that he had had as little choice as she. Nor did she at heart resent him for the boast that had caused her predicament. Boasting was in his nature, the only vice he possessed amongst a multitude of virtues. She did not wish to return to her impoverished state nor reduce her parents to their old privations, yet she missed much of the simple life she had led among good people with common sense.

Now married, she could not un-marry and must suffer the humiliation of being surrounded by those who looked down on her. But she swore that her child would never grow up to disdain her mother or her grandparents or the other hardworking folk of their class, and she took the Princess Pearl often to visit the mill and the two-room cottage which was the only place the Queen could feel genuinely at home.

و

Inevitably, the King and Queen grew further and further apart as the years went by. The King began to enjoy himself with ladies of the court while Queen Elsa and her daughter spent more and more time at the homes of her parents and of her former neighbors. At every opportunity she encouraged her daughter's friendships with the village girls, and praised the honesty, industriousness, and wholesome vigor of the boys, lecturing Pearl from childhood on the superiority of the trading and peasant classes. As the Princess Pearl approached marriageable age, Queen Elsa was determined to prevent her from marrying a haughty, supercilious nobleman.

When Pearl was sixteen, her father began to consider appropriate suitors for her. Elsa's heart chilled when she heard of his choices: A wealthy prince known for a ferocious dedication to the hunt and a fondness for sending his vassals into war. A rich young earl with such a predilection for red meat and champagne that already at the age of twenty-five he suffered from gouty ankles.

Fortunately, Pearl did not take an interest in her father's choices. She had learned well, her mother thought, to prefer the yellow in a plain bale of straw to the gold in a nobleman's waistcoat. When Pearl turned eighteen, however, the situation grew dire, for the King was fast losing his health and wanted to see his daughter well married before he died. The Princess Pearl, as his only child, would rule after his death. It was essential, he asserted, that she marry a man of the highest birth, since Pearl's husband would be the consort of her reign.

Now it happened that there was a young man of the village, a blacksmith's son, whom the princess had played with as a child and had come to love. Her mother told her, "This is the man you shall marry."

The Queen now hatched a plan. She told the King, "Since the superiority of our daughter's husband is of critical importance, I propose we open the field to all eligible noblemen and then put the various suitors to a test." The King approved this idea and proposed contests of physical prowess—horsemanship, archery, and the like. But the Queen reminded him that the princess as monarch would be well protected by her palace guards, knights and army. It was superior intellect, not physical prowess that she would need in a husband. A man who by his wits could help her maintain her protectors' allegiance. The Queen recommended a test of intelligence.

The King agreed, and in the infirmity of his illness, left it to her to devise the test. She told him that if gold could be spun from straw by a mere peasant girl, straw could certainly be extracted from gold by a clever and resourceful prince. This would be the task to which they would set the noble suitors.

⌇

Some weeks prior to this discussion with the King, Queen Elsa had asked her courier discreetly as to the whereabouts of the bandy-legged little gnome, Rumpelstiltskin. Upon being directed to his lair in the hollow of an ancient tree, she called upon the fellow in secret.

"I would like you to tell me how straw might be extracted from gold," she said. The little man glared at her and replied, "You see the dismal pass I have come to, living alone and uncared for in the trunk of a tree?" He shook his dingy beard, now grown very long and gray, and cried, "Why should I help you after you deprived me of a daughter to comfort me in my old age?"

"The King is gravely ill and will die soon," the Queen replied. "My daughter, the princess, will succeed him. Should the peasant man whom she loves perform such a feat as turning gold into straw, he will win her hand, and if that occurs, their reign and that of their offspring will always be distinguished by the deepest respect and consideration for the poor and humble."

The gnome sneered. "Oh yes, I like the sound of that," he

said. "It sounds like heaven indeed. But the rich and power-ful make promises they easily squirm out of," he said. "What guarantee have I that what you promise will transpire?"

The Queen was so confident of the loyalties she had instilled in her daughter and of the worthiness of Pearl's peasant suitor that she promised without hesitation, "If what I say does not come to pass, you may have my daughter's first born child to comfort you in your old age." At that, the gnome agreed and whispered the magic word in her ear.

On the day of the great contest, forty young noblemen lined up in the palace courtyard to hear how they would be tested. At the end of the line was the blacksmith's son, resplendent in the princely raiment provided him by the Queen to disguise his simple origins. When the Queen gave the men their task, one by one the suitors unwound the gold threads from their bobbins and mightily pulled and stretched and pounded them, but the threads remained gold.

Finally, the disguised peasant youth stepped forth, scratch-ing under his bejeweled collar, for he was unused to such stiff attire. He held his bobbin lightly in his hand, then with a flash of his wrist, spun the gold threads loose, whispering three times in succession the word Queen Elsa had given him: *Nikstlislepmur! Nikstlislepmur! Nikstlislepmur!* And there, before the eyes of the astonished court, appeared a sturdy sheaf of yellow straw neatly tied with gold thread.

On the spot, the King betrothed the young man to his daughter and sent the other suitors away. The wedding took place within the week. Only after the ceremony did the King learn of his son-in-law's humble lineage. The discovery may well have hastened the King's demise, for two months hence, despite the happy news that he was soon to have a grandchild, he breathed his last.

The Queen Mother bore a faint, lingering tenderness for the departed King and was wistful for some weeks. But her mood lightened each time she saw her daughter's peasant husband dining with them at the royal table and her own parents invited to the palace on state occasions. She looked forward to the long, just, and beneficent reign of Pearl and her consort.

It was with misgiving then, and a trickle of icy fear, that the Queen Mother observed something new in the behavior of her daughter. At supper in the royal banquet hall one evening, she heard the young queen laugh at her husband's awkward attempts to peel his fruit. Pearl took the fruit from his hands and showed him how to peel it properly. Then she leaned toward him and, with a little sneer, chided him for having lengthened the vowel on the third syllable of the word *pomegranate*.

THE EMPEROR'S PROCESSION

Shivering at his chamber window, the Emperor acknowledged to himself
that clothes were his weakness. Diplomats from other imperial
houses knew how to seal treaties with him, not by offering
gold ingots but silk, damask, leopard's fur and ostrich plumes.
Yet this weakness was due not to vanity, but to shame.

When the foreign tailors had dressed him from head to foot,
they bowed deeply and proclaimed him the most splendidly
clad monarch they'd had the honor to behold. "Only to those
unfortunates who are unfit for their duties in life will your
magnificent suit be invisible. Pity those who will be deprived
of this glorious sight." And they held the mirror in front of
him so he could admire their handiwork.

The Emperor hid his dismay at seeing himself naked, for it
confirmed his suspicion that he was not fit for his own office.
"At least," thought he, "the majority will see me in a splendid
suit of clothes, and those few for whom it is invisible will not
dare to say so and expose their own deficiencies." Thus he
comforted himself.

Still, as the procession began to assemble and he felt the
dank palace vapors upon his bare skin and the stone floor
chilling the bones of his feet, he felt uneasy. "Suppose," he
fretted, "that some inebriated fool—a failed merchant or in-

competent carpenter—in a moment of drunken recklessness blurts a description of my person!" At this thought, his palms on the window casing grew clammy with fear.

His inherited imperfections of proportion, as well as the effects of too much rich food, were all too evident to him. Whenever he faced his reflection in the looking glass, he saw that his various parts lacked proper length, height and girth. Some parts were spindly, others ungainly and rotund. He was, in fact, homely and inelegant and was afraid that as man and monarch he cut so poor a figure, one so deficient in the symmetry, coloring and grace of a true emperor, that anyone who saw him would deem him unfit to wear a crown.

ﯨ

But now it was time for the march to begin and the Emperor must put this worry aside. He drew a long breath to expand his flaccid chest. With all the dignity of his position, he held his head high and descended to the palace courtyard, where he took his place under the royal canopy. The imperial guards and noble lords and ladies who were to precede him were already in their ranks, facing the palace gates. The Emperor noticed that when he passed the company of soldiers who waited to bring up the rear, and approached the four pairs of footmen who held the canopy under which he would walk, all seemed to forget their duties for a moment as he came into view, and stood open-mouthed before abruptly pulling themselves to attention.

The procession commenced. The Emperor heard the hollow clop of horses' hooves and the enormous gates creaking open. Ahead, he heard the crowd break into thunderous cheers and applause as his palace guards rode out on horses bedecked with banners and as the elegant courtiers followed onto the cobbled street.

Finally, the yellow silk canopy, held high over the Emperor by satin-clad attendants, approached the gate. There was a seething crush of people hoping for the chance to see him. They jostled each other and shouted back and forth. Children frolicked. At the sight of the yellow flags and tassels blowing in the breeze, the crowd raised their cheers higher and pressed closer. Parents pushed their children to the front. "You may never have another chance to see so fine a spectacle," said one father to his son as they surged forward with the crowd. At these words, the Emperor forgot his misgivings and his heart swelled with pride. His raiments—the tailors had assured him—were finer than any worn by monarchs at the courts of Araby or Cathay and would evoke in his subjects awe and eternal allegiance.

Now when he came fully into the crowd's sight, the cheering suddenly subsided and the onlookers fell silent. As the Emperor walked gravely and majestically past, not a single sound was uttered, though mouths gaped like those of fishes gasping in the bottom of a boat, and eyes stared as wide as cats' eyes probing the dark.

The hush daunted the Emperor for a moment, but he thought to himself, "Well, my clothes are so fine that the populace is struck dumb." And he puffed his chest out more and held his chin higher and slowed his pace, so that no one might be deprived of the sight of him. At every turning, the throngs fell silent and the procession made its way in such solemnity that, but for the sound of hooves and boots upon the cobbles and the flap of the canopy in the breeze, one might have been able to hear an ant cross from one side of the road to the other.

Then out of this silence came a high, piping laugh, the clapping of small hands, and the clear voice of a very young girl. "The Emperor is naked!" From the corner of his eye, the Emperor spied the girl atop her father's shoulders. The father shushed her, swung her down, and pushed her to the back. But her little voice rang out again from behind him. "Look, Papa!" she cried, "Look, Mama! The Emperor is not wearing any clothes!"

Then on all sides the Emperor heard a stirring and murmuring and whispering. Though the lords and ladies who walked ahead of him and the foot soldiers bringing up the rear kept silent, the throngs on either side of the street were quoting the child's words in low tones and passing them along before and behind. The full truth of the little girl's declaration struck him like the first rock hurled at a wretch awaiting death by stoning. At that moment he knew he had been fooled, and was a fool, and was exposed for a fool—an ill-proportioned, pathetic, and grotesque fool at that—wearing only the covering he was born with.

There on the street he stopped and stood as if at his looking-glass in the privacy of his chambers, seeing what he had never allowed another to see. And the looking-glass reflected back a thousand images of his squat, round-shouldered, bandy-legged figure.

The Emperor and his entourage quickened their gait but could not outpace the news running on before them like a wave on the incoming tide. Soon the procession turned a corner into the open cathedral square. Here the intercut of streets slowed the spread of the news, and the procession hurried across the open space as if driven from behind. In the middle of the square, the Emperor felt his heart race, his eyes dim. His breath came short and for a moment he slowed his steps and the soldiers behind almost overran him as his footmen continued to carry the canopy forward. On all sides the crowd loomed like a huge, thousand-eyed monster.

The Emperor was aware that every despised part of his ignominious body was under the scrutiny of those eyes. His spindly legs, protruding like sticks under his pendulous belly. The rounded, narrow shoulders, wattled neck, flabby, caved chest, and doughy buttocks. Pulling himself straight to tighten his belly did nothing to improve his appearance and only revealed the inconsiderable private parts hidden under his belly's fold.

The Emperor could not fathom what to do next, other than continue onward, for if he reversed his course, what then? Like a weak and pathetic army walking away from a mighty foe, there was no way to turn back without a worse disgrace.

The rhythmic stamp of feet upon the stone resounded sharply from the buildings bordering the square, recalling to the Emperor the ceremonious march of prisoners across those same stones to the public gallows. In the shade of the canopy the Emperor felt cold. Gooseflesh blossomed down his naked back and arms. He could not control his shivering.

Then from opposite corners of the square, he heard more children's voices lisp the innocent words, "Look, look, the Emperor is naked!" "See! He has nothing on!" The crowd craned its multitude of necks to get a better view, and again voices whispered and swirled around him.

Across the square and into the broad street the procession forged on. The Emperor could not see the faces of the noble ladies and lords marching ahead, but he thought their shoulders trembled with suppressed laughter. Beyond them he caught glimpses of an exaggerated rigidity in the backs of the mounted guards, as if only extreme discipline prevented explosions of mirth. The Emperor dared not let his gaze fall to the right or left of him for fear of the amusement and scorn he would find in the faces of the crowd.

Struggling to maintain on his own face an expression of dignity and inscrutability, he achieved only a look of grim endurance. His mouth was dry, his jaw clenched, his teeth ground together, his eyes focused inward. The bottoms of his feet were scraped and bruised where sharp pebbles bore into the tender naked soles. But he dared not allow himself to be seen prancing and capering to avoid them.

At every new turning another child called out with naive curiosity, "Why does the Emperor go naked?" or with innocent merriment, "How funny the Emperor looks without clothes."

On and on the Emperor and his entourage continued, up one crowded street and down another, past taverns, inns, shops and the houses of merchants, jammed with folk leaning from balconies and windows. They stared slack-jawed in astonishment, as if they could not believe what they saw.

The Emperor began to feel that he was sleepwalking and was trapped in some terrible dream. The pageantry of the procession appeared fantastic and over-bright, the muttering voices like the ominous and incomprehensible murmurings of creatures in nightmares. He shivered still, but no longer felt the cold wind on his flesh, for his body had gone numb, while his mind boiled with fancies and desperate schemes.

Though all the world knew now that he had been fooled, he could not acknowledge the disgrace. At any cost he must maintain the pretence of majesty and find a way to escape his humiliation. Perhaps he could order broadsides to be posted throughout the land condemning traitors for goading their innocent children into telling lies. He would offer rewards for those who brought the treacherous mothers and fathers to justice. Or he could let it be known that those who thought they saw the Emperor naked were victims of sorcery. An ugly and wicked magician, to settle an old grievance, had implanted the image of the magician's own naked body into the eyes of the Emperor's onlookers.

Many such rash and reckless stratagems ran through the Emperor's mind as he trudged on, yet he knew he was grasping at straws. Nothing would hide the truth now that it was abroad. In street after street came the shouts and giggles of children. "Where is the wonderful suit, Papa?" "He forgot to put on his clothes!" "Look! The Emperor is such a funny old man!" With every step, he longed to pull down the billowing yellow canopy he walked beneath and wrap it around himself like a great enveloping robe.

The procession neared the city gates. Crowds of strapping, swaggering young men had climbed to the top of the walls for a clear view. As soon as they caught sight of the Emperor and heard the children crying the truth below, they clapped their hands over their mouths and bent double with gasps and chokings of laughter. Several of them came near to tumbling off the wall in their hilarity and had to be hauled back from the edge by their fellows. Rage rose within the Emperor's heart. "I will order every one of these arrogant blackguards to be seized!" he thought, furiously. "With one word to my guards, these insolent knaves will find themselves pulled down, stripped of their clothes and run through with swords. Then see how they hold their stomachs, to keep not mirth but life's blood from spilling onto the street. Then see how their jolly expressions turn ghastly on their disembodied heads lined up along the wall!"

These wrathful thoughts consumed the Emperor's mind, yet he could not bring himself to command his guards, for he would have to suffer their turning around to look at him. And would they obey the command of the rotund little naked figure that he was now? He feared they would not.

The Emperor's cogitations continued to torment him as he passed through the gate and out into the open countryside. Here, unchecked by the buildings of the town, the cold wind afflicted him tenfold. No one would dare to offer him a wrap, and he could not ask for one, so he shivered on, his teeth chattering wildly like Romany castanets. His bare feet bled now, cut by rocks and rubble. But at least, here on the rural highway, the crowd was thinner. In the gaps, incurious pigs and chickens went about their business of rooting and pecking, unaware that a shameful spectacle passed them by. The peasantry stood in stolid consternation, their hats in their hands. Their children were more obedient than those of liberal townfolk. Here, when the little ones opened their mouths to speak, their elders were quick to tap them sharply on their heads lest they forget that children were to be seen and not heard.

And so the long procession went more silently than in town, except for the blowing wind and the tinkle of bells on the necks of ruminating cows and goats. In the open countryside, surrounded by far-reaching hills and fields and under the vast sky with its scudding clouds, the Emperor was overcome with loneliness. As if he had other eyes to look on himself from afar, he saw how small and pitiful and friendless he was, stripped not just of clothing but of solace. An Emperor, yet with no loyal comrades to step forward and take his humiliation onto their shoulders, no mothering soul to soothe and sympathize, no defender to come forth and chasten the contemptuous crowd. Not even an avenging God to strike them down.

Though surrounded by his subjects, high and low, he walked

entirely alone, and knew he had ever been alone, though he had never realized it before, and would always be alone henceforth. He imagined himself walking on, when they arrived at the place where the procession was to turn back. Walking and walking until he came to a forest, there to lie down and die. No one would mourn him. His only legacy would be the tale of his humiliation, a legend told around firesides by aged granddames and patriarchs. "I saw it with my own eyes!" they would boast. "Though I was but three years old, I remember clearly that I spoke these very words: 'Papa, the Emperor is naked!' " Then the gathered audience would remember how the Emperor had been swindled and made a fool of, and made to look worse than a fool!

The Emperor could hear the laughter around the fireside as clearly as if it were happening that very moment instead of in the distant future, and now he had to face the next ordeal to come in the present, for the procession must soon walk the five miles back. No doubt the populace would still be waiting, having spent the intervening hours relishing and discussing his shame and eager for another sight of him, purple with gooseflesh and hobbling on bare, wounded feet. There would be much debate about his fitness for rule. If he survived this gauntlet, and finally reached the palace, how then would he retain the loyalty of his subjects? His empire would collapse and he would be banished or imprisoned.

An old abbey was now in sight, a cluster of peasant cottages and animal pens huddled against its ruined walls. The population of the little settlement waited at the roadside with posies in hand ready to toss at the Emperor's feet. The clothing of these simple folk had been made as clean and tidy as tattered clothes could be. Even the animals' coats had been brushed free of dust. As the guards and nobles approached and passed, the thin crowd watched respectfully and threw their flowers at the Emperor's canopy when it rounded the mile post marking the distance from the abbey back to town.

The Emperor looked grimly upon the dumbfounded, uncertain stares the crowd cast upon him when he came into view. His shoulders, bent now in exhaustion, tightened and narrowed in expectation of some child's cry, for there were more children here than it was in the parents' power to control. Suddenly the inevitable cry came and the Emperor cringed at it. Then, a tiny girl, ignoring restraining hands, broke from her mother's grasp. She toddled down a ditch, scurried onto the road and came to a stop in front of the Emperor, forcing him to halt and his foot soldiers to pile up again behind him.

Making a polite curtsy—as best she could, for she was but four or five years old—she admonished the Emperor earnestly. "Your Majesty," said she, "we mustn't go outside without our clothes on. Ma says we'll catch cold if we do!" And she took off her brown, homespun cloak and held it up for him to put on. In fascination, the people of the Emperor's entourage at last turned to look directly at him. But he did not notice. He lowered himself slowly to his knees in the dusty road and took the little cloak from the child's hands. For some seconds he gazed at it, unseeing, running his fingers along the coarse weave absently, as though deep in thought. The little girl waited in respectful silence. At last he spoke to her.

"My dear child," he said in a serious yet tender voice, "it would be an honor for an emperor to wear such a fine cloak." He looked into her earnest eyes and smiled. "But the sun shines so brightly today that I have decided to return to town not under the shade of this canopy but enjoying the full measure of the sun's warmth on my skin. Thus, you see, I shall not be cold." Gently, he placed the cloak around her small shoulders. "I am much obliged to you, my child, but I think it best that you keep your lovely cloak." The child made him another curtsy, then skipped back across the ditch to her mother, who grasped her by the hand and stared at the Emperor in wonder.

Now the Emperor rose and brushed the dust from his knees. Ceremoniously, he stepped out from under his canopy and turned to face the assemblage—the guards and nobles and foot soldiers, the peasants beside the road, the dogs frisking in and out among their legs, and the sheep and pigs poking their noses through their pens. The Emperor raised his eyes to the enormous blue sky and bright sun, and thence across the wide green fields and hills. He turned in the direction from which the wind was blowing and let it sweep over his naked chest and stomach and legs and arms and caress his bare, bald pate. Finally, he turned to his entourage again and looked frankly into the eyes of the captain of his guards. "Now," he commanded him. "Let us return!" The captain saluted smartly and called the order to his mounted men. His lieutenant, in turn, swung his horse around and shouted the order over the heads of the noble lords and ladies, to the imperial company of foot soldiers. Then, with slow and solemn dignity, the great procession turned and marched back toward the town.

THE RED CHAMBER AND
THE BLUE CHAMBER

One bright summer afternoon, a wicked sorcerer entered an apothecary shop to buy poisonous herbs. Soon after, another entered on the same errand. On seeing the nature of each other's purchases, they introduced themselves.

"Mr. Pernicious Baneblight, at your service," said the one. He was a lean, drowsy-looking figure, wearing a tall hat and brindle cape rather too long and heavy for such a warm day but concealing a number of charms and small dessicated animals suspended from the waist of his doublet. Bowing low, he sneaked a look at the amulets inside the other's pockets.

"Madame Vindicta Pox-Take-You," replied the second, a haggard crone of pursed lips and perpetual glare. She slid a hand across her pocket opening while memorizing the runic inscriptions woven into the crown of the other's hat. Arching an eyebrow at him, she said, "So pleased to make your acquaintance, Mr. Baneblight. I see you have purchased a packet of monkshood. Personally, I favor larkspur for its deceptive beauty. It apes the deep blue color of a sky in midsummer, making it most effective for luring those susceptible to the presumed glories of nature." She made an expansive professorial gesture, almost striking the other in the face. "By draping garlands of larkspur prettily along a stone staircase," she boasted, "I drew a child to the highest room of a tall tower and locked her in without once resorting to magic."

Mr. Baneblight's eyelids drooped with affected indifference. "I suppose larkspur has its merits," he conceded, "but monkshood is of an equally deep shade of blue—with, I will venture to say, more enticing blooms—while being quicker-acting and more lethal to human beings. Larkspur is fit only for poisoning cattle."

The crone was about to dispute this claim, when the shop bell rang and a third sorcerer entered, carrying a basketful of sweets and other gifts tied up with gay ribbons and sprigs of rosemary. Her sparkling black eyes were almost lost in the plumpness of her cheeks, which betrayed a habit of smiling. The dress she wore was extravagantly festooned with bows and flounces and swept the floor as she walked.

"Good morning!" she greeted the two in passing. At the counter she spoke cordially to the shopkeeper. "If you please," she said, "three pennyworth each of..." she consulted her list "...comfrey, camomile, blessed thistle, angelica root and star flower." She placed fifteen pennies on the counter, and the apothecary went off to fill her order.

Madame Pox-Take-You drew her companion aside and muttered to him in an undertone. "That" she said, "is Mistress Do-Good. A more interfering busybody you will never meet."

"How so?" inquired her companion.

"Without so much as a by-your-leave, that creature mitigated a vengeful curse of mine, which I had pronounced with the utmost justification."

"You don't say. Tell me the story."

"I was excluded from my own goddaughter's christening by her parents, the King and Queen. So, of course, I had to condemn the princess—"

"—Naturally," interjected her listener.

"—to die of a pricked finger upon reaching her sixteenth birthday—"

"—A fitting curse, I should say—"

"—I thought so—"

"But—?"

"This interloper—" she stared stonily at the figure standing by the counter, "—altered the sentence to one hundred years of sleep and the awakening kiss of a prince!"

"Abominable," Mr. Baneblight commiserated. "The same sort of thing happened to me. I once rendered a young woman barren—the reason escapes me for the moment—and no sooner did she and her husband reach old age (when, by rights, they should have lived miserably without consolation of kith or kin), than a meddlesome magician conjured them a daughter the size of a thumb!"

His companion shook her head. "It should not be allowed. A curse is a curse."

"And a spell a spell."

The two stared balefully at the beribboned sorcerer who had bent for a moment to sniff a jar of rose petals on a shelf. "There are two standards," grumbled the crone. "One for us. One for them. And all in their favor."

"These so-called *good* spells cannot be modified!"—the sorcerer was becoming uncustomarily exercised—"While an evil spell can be abridged and attenuated in all manner of ways by any wisewoman or witch-healer—whatever they call themselves—who takes a fancy to do so. It is unjust, I say!" His cadaverous complexion had turned an apoplectic mauve.

Mistress Do-Good could not help overhearing this last sentence, spoken with such vehemence, and came quickly forward. The idea of injustice always aroused in her an urgency to put things right. "My colleagues," she said, "of what injustice do you complain?"

"Well may you ask, Mistress One-Hundred-Years-Of-Sleep," sneered the first sorcerer.

"Oh, I see who you are now, Madame Pox-Take-You. Please forgive my slighting you. I am a most absent-minded body and had my thoughts on healing herbs today." She laughed merrily at her own foible.

The other sorcerer folded his cloak more tightly around his spare frame to restrain his wand, which was agitated with an eagerness to strike the plump fairy a blow. "The likes of you, who constantly fetter us in the practice of our arts," he muttered through clenched teeth, "*you* are the ones who commit the injustice we speak of."

The fairy godmother—for such was Mistress Do-Good—considered his complaint. "On the face of it, our intervention would seem to be unfair," said she, "but if you compare the different natures of our spells—forgiving, on the one hand, and vindictive, on the other—the law clearly—"

"The law should be abolished!" Madame Pox-Take-You exclaimed.

"It is immutable."

"By whose decree?"

"By nature's, of course. Good must triumph over evil."

Mr. Baneblight laughed scornfully, but his companion exploded in fury. "It is an outrage!" screamed Madame Pox-Take-You. Doors and windows in the little shop banged open and closed of their own accord and mice scurried from the walls and scampered back and forth in a state of confusion.

"There, there," said Mistress Do-Good, upon which the doors and windows quietly returned to their original positions and the mice to their slumbers. "Let us not speak in such a contentious manner. Perhaps some sort of assembly should be called to discuss the matter further. Representatives from both sides might—"

"A congress of magicians," reflected the second sorcerer. "To settle the question for once and all." He pondered the idea for a moment.

"Have no doubt which way it would go!" shrieked his companion to Mistress Do-Good. "Our numbers and powers are greater by far than those of your persuasion."

"Very well," said Mistress Do-Good, feeling a little stimulated by the challenge. "We shall meet."

And so it was agreed that they would summon their sisters and brothers in the magic arts—good and evil—to take up the question. Word went out that very day on the four winds. Delegates were duly elected on both sides, and a fortnight later the congress commenced.

ॐ

The assembly was held in a great hall composed of two magnificent chambers each entered by way of a separate atrium. The rooms on one side were draped in the deep purplish-blue color of a sky at eventide. Those on the other side were mantled in the bright scarlet of freshly spilled blood. Over the arched doorway of the Red Chamber's Atrium, the word "Malevolent" was etched in marble. On the Blue side was engraved the word "Benevolent." Under these two entablatures there passed hundreds of magic makers, who had arrived in small boats that plied the narrow canals leading up to the hall.

Plump Mistress Do-Good and her eleven stout sisters bustled into the Blue Atrium, laden with pouches of healing herbs to be distributed without bias to anyone for whom the proceedings became too taxing. Madame Pox-Take-You, reaching the Red door at the same time, cast a withering glance at the sisters and, with eyes darting about in search of allies, hurried into the Red Atrium. Behind her, a cohort of goblins pushed and shoved with sharp elbows to get through the door. These were followed by a swaggering group of imps, who cackled at the sight of the goblins' backsides and passed uncouth jests at their expense, causing several skirmishes, which were aggravated in great part by a heavy gilt mirror entering the Red Atrium on the back of a scowling queen.

"Make haste," the mirror scolded its bearer. "Thou art swift, but others are far more swift than thee." And as the disgruntled queen bore the heavy mirror along, the thing accosted everyone it passed with divisive jibes, spoken in tones of mock sympathy: "*Thou* art *middling* fair, but *he* is fairer still," "Thou art glib and brazenfaced enough, but *they* are *cunning*, as well," and so forth.

There was a rancorous dispute when a bearded Piper passed through the Red Atrium and tried to enter the Red Chamber without first leaving his magic instrument at the door. The matter was finally settled when he agreed to wear the pipe sheathed and tied by a string around his neck, where all had a view of it dangling on his chest and could scatter if he made a move to unsheath it.

Meanwhile, in the Blue Atrium there was much polite greeting, exchanging of news and sharing of useful lore, all of which delayed entry and seating in the Blue Chamber. Finally, the fairies, fairy godmothers, wood- and water-sprites, brownies, witch healers and other benign sorcerers took their places a full hour past the appointed time.

The two chambers were separated by a magic curtain, which now withdrew to open the rooms into a lofty, bi-colored hall divided by an aisle down the center. Elevated on a dais at the front of the hall were seated a tribunal of six sorcerers, who had been elected to take charge of the proceedings—Goody Treatwell, Master Loosepurse, and Mistress Makepeace for the Blue side and Mistress Lackmercy, Master Grasp-All, and Master Tit-Tat for the Red. All six had been chosen for their venerable age and experience.

While these six sorcerers presided on the dais, in the great hall below sat an assemblage of several hundred other magic makers, wicked and good. Goblins and imps had arrived in such great numbers and were so uncontrollable that they were consigned to the gallery where they looked on from above. Arguments hissed back and forth among them whether or not to return a stolen baby whom they were desultorily nursing. Now that the fretful infant was proving to be more trouble than they had bargained for, some wanted to return it and release the changeling they had left in its place.

On the Blue side of the Gallery, overseen by a bevy of bemused sprites, a dozen brownies were keeping busy making shoes on behalf of a poor shoemaker. The tap of their little hammers mingled with the sniggering of the goblins across the way, who leaned over the rail to taunt them: "Idle hands the devil's playground, eh?" The brownies paid little heed. While their nimble fingers hammered and stitched, their minds were on the serious business taking place in the hall below.

ॐ

At last one blue and one red gavel came down, and the question was put before the assembly. Master Tit-Tat rose with a clang and squeak of steel. He affected a lavishly etched and gilded suit of armor from head to toe, including a steel breastplate and a helmet whose visor was continually falling shut. This, mercifully, concealed his gloating smirk and narrowed, suspicious eyes, leaving only slits through which he observed and remarked on the proceedings. He read aloud the Red side's opening statement in a caustic voice uncannily magnified inside the hollow cavity of his helmet, like the mutterings of a nocturnal ghost echoing along a castle corridor: "We challenge the right of benevolent sorcerers to frustrate by annulment, restriction, interdiction or nullification, the full execution of a spell cast with malevolent intent. And we propose that a law be declared against the practice."

When he sat down, Mistress Makepeace stood. She was wrinkled with age and as humpbacked as a dromedary. Her only adornment was a plain white ruff attached to a simple gown of gray, which matched her alert gray eyes. On her brow a mild furrow of concentration gave her the expression of one who has spent a lifetime attending with interest to all that is said and done around her. She now began to explain the Blue side's position: "Just as an apple falls *down* from a branch—never *up*—it is a law of nature that good must triumph over evil—"

This preamble brought the Red side to its feet in a fury, and the ensuing argument required the better part of the morning before rules for maintaining order could be settled on. Finally, Mistress Makepeace was allowed to continue, thus: "The fairness of tempering a harmful spell has been challenged by our malevolent colleagues. Regarding this point, we wish to come to an amicable agreement which will promote understanding and harmony among us. And perhaps, while we are all here convened, we might take up other questions as well, such as—"

"On no account," interrupted Mistress Lackmercy. Her voice sliced through the other's speech like a surgeon's blade through flesh. "We will not debate trivial and extraneous matters." The wiry old woman wore a gown of scabrous green, which clung to her body like a snake's skin. One side of her upper lip seemed permanently fixed in a curled position, until her mouth suddenly opened as now into a fervid and cruel smile, revealing white teeth, chiseled to points. "The question is, can you or can you not alter a spell once cast—"

"Can't!" shrieked a chorus of goblins and imps from the gallery, dissolving into idiotic cackles, which annoyed even their own allies on the Red side of the hall.

"Very well," said Mistress Makepeace, in a conciliatory tone. "We will limit the discussion to this one topic." And so the testimony began.

᠊ᢒ

Madame Pox-Take-You was the first to be called. She reminded the assembly of the grievance she held toward Sleeping Beauty and her parents. Puzzled, Master Loosepurse remarked, "Good Madame, by what reasoning do you claim ascendancy for your evil christening gift when the child had twelve blessings from twelve fairy godmothers against your one curse?"

She turned a look of disdain on the bouncing, portly little fellow, almost completely bald except for two cottony tufts protruding above his ears. His well-worn, rather shoddy suit of clothes was encumbered by capacious and overstuffed pockets, from which he distributed licorice lozenges, shawls, handkerchiefs, foodstuffs and all manner of other things which delegates may have forgotten to bring along. He now offered Madame Pox-Take-You a small Oriental fan, for her face was quite flushed from anger, but she ignored the gesture, turning her back on him to address the fairy godmothers, who sat knitting and tatting in the first row, their generous hips impinging upon each other like cabbages planted too close together. "Have any of you suffered the outrage that I did?" Madame Pox-Take-You accused.

Mistress Do-Good put down her knitting and replied soothingly, "To be sure, Sister, we sympathize with you regarding the injured feelings which you suffered, yet recall earlier incidents in which you did not behave in quite a trustworthy manner. Perhaps you can see why the King and Queen would not have wanted—"

"Blast 'injured feelings'! It's nothing to do with injured feelings! It is the principle of the thing."

At this, Mistress Makepeace, in her quiet, reasoned voice, posed a theoretical question. "Perhaps we should consider if one negative should hold the power of veto against twelve positives."

"It should and must!" asserted Master Grasp-All in his booming, insistent voice, which none could ignore. He stood up. A tall, broad-shouldered fellow, bearded and only a little stooped in old age, he commanded a great deal of space on the dais. His ample robes were adorned with every sort of precious gem and costly fur under the sun, as if he hadn't been able to decide from among them, and so, elected to wear them all. "The scale has ever been unfairly tipped in favor of your so-called benevolent spells," he declared, "while we are deprived of the right to sufficiently chasten greedy and corrupt mortals—"

A surge of noise from the gallery drowned the rest of his words. Caught up in the excitement of the debate, the brownies had inadvertently increased the vigor of their work, wielding their little tack hammers as if they were mallets. The goblins, on their side, were trying to quiet the stolen baby by shaking it, which caused it to cry all the harder. Then a wood sprite crossed the gallery aisle and snatched the infant from its goblin caretaker, almost precipitating a battle. But fortunately, the sight of the becalmed and comforted child reminded the goblins of how glad they were to have the troublesome thing off their hands, and they contented themselves only with shouting lecherous insults at the sprite (and sprites in general) until a gavel below came down forcefully, and proceedings continued.

On the dais, Mistress Makepeace called the next speaker, the necromancer who had turned a prince into a pig. The evil sorcerer was indignant. "My point," he said, "is that no good ever comes from mitigating a harsh sentence. I, myself, moderated my own spell, with disastrous consequences, even without the meddling of a do-good sorcerer. Not from any kindness of heart," he reassured his startled sisters and brothers on the Red side, "but from curiosity only, and you see what the outcome was? The Prince learned nothing by the penalty of beasthood until I could reinstate it upon his wife. Without an adequately harsh consequence to his action, he would neither have refrained from poaching again nor learned to value the love of a so-called 'good' woman—" The goblins' sniggering at this juncture forced a momentary pause in the testimony.

"But good fellow," put in Master Loosepurse, "the Prince did not realize the boar was yours."

"Not realize?!" retorted the sorcerer. "What of it?! Were it I who poached the Prince's boar instead of the other way around, can you doubt I would be rotting, as we speak, in his dismal dungeons or, worse, hanging from his gallows, my eyes plucked out by carrion birds, my words '*I didn't realize…*' cast like ghosts upon the wind?" His colleagues on the Red side nodded, knowingly. "Nay," he concluded, "turning him into a beast was merciful compared to what his royal highness would have done to me."

"But then," inquired Goody Treatwell, "why punish the Princess?" A nimbus of frizzy white curls floated around her kind old face, from which radiated an expression of such tenderness that all but the most hard-hearted must find themselves wishing to climb into her lap and nestle against her accommodating bosom. Her fingers idly stroked a long-haired tabby who, under the inestimably gentle caress, purred loudly enough to be heard in the highest row of the gallery. "Young Beauty's only crime was to offer the Prince the very love you had made provision for," she said. Her deepset brown eyes, the color of melting chocolate, filled with tears of compassion.

" 'Only crime' ?! Did you not hear how your precious Beauty capitulated to her impulse for revenge in the end?"

"Only after you tried her to the limit of her endurance and brought out the worst in the poor child."

"Precisely so, for they all have a worst side to bring out. And did I not teach the pair a lesson in humility that may slightly improve their chance for a place on a higher ring of Hell in the afterlife?"

The whole of the Red Chamber leapt to its feet, roaring approval. Their applause thundered to such heights it set all the crystal chandeliers tinkling. The goblins, from pure enthusiasm and with their usual indiscriminate impulsiveness, leaned over the gallery rail and poured flagons of ale upon the heads below, dousing a section of demons, who flew up and sprang upon the mischief makers, causing serious injury to several. When this melee had been brought to a conclusion and wounds magically excised, the next testimony went forward.

This was from none other than the fairy godmother to the unfortunate Cinderella, old Mother Cuddle Up. She was a neat, unassuming little body with gray hair in a tidy bun and the round blue eyes of a kitten. The good sorcerer reminded her listeners that her own benevolent spells were always thwarted by arbitrary time constraints. "I, too" said she, "am hindered in the practice of my magic—and this without the intervention of any other sorcerer. My spells, by custom, last but two hours. Poor Cinderella, for instance, was required to end her evening so abruptly that she lost a shoe! So, you see, we too are sometimes frustrated, yet I do not complain and think it is often for the best—"

"Perhaps, Mother Muddle-It-Up, midnight was not the most intelligent curfew you might have imposed upon your little scullery maid," interrupted Master Tit-Tat, with a bland, mocking smile. "Was it due to your extravagant world-wise-ness that you imagined engagement balls of the aristocracy which commence at the hour of ten are likely to end before midnight?" He eyed the room as a jester surveys his court audience and was rewarded with appreciative titters from the Red side. On the face of every Blue Chamber occupant was an expression of sympathy and alarm on behalf of their humiliated sister. Master Tit-Tat continued, "Perhaps in your dotage, midnight seems a very late hour indeed."

The target of his derision faced him with a slight tremor in her voice. "Yet had Cinderella stayed longer," said she, "there would have been no chance for the Prince to prove his love." The Red side exploded with laughter.

"Indeed," jeered Master Tit-Tat, "and we recall how *that* turned out!" Old Mother Cuddle Up blushed. Mistress Make-peace brought down her gavel.

"It is time," she announced, "to confer with our commit-tees." And the magic curtain swept unceremoniously down the aisle from ceiling to floor, with a gossamer rustling like the faintest of sighs, thus cloistering the two chambers from each other.

In order to conduct the business of the congress more efficiently, sorcerers of like minds and temperaments had formed themselves into small deputations or committees. These now met in clusters scattered about the separate chambers.

On the Red side, Master Tit-Tat was joined by the Pied Piper, the Magic Mirror, and the sorcerer, Master Peevish, who had turned a prince into a pig. This group was the only Red committee that achieved some measure of success. Though hindered in their work by petulant quarrels over who was the most notorious ("*I* am more infamous by far," the Magic Mirror insisted), they still were able to compose a list of rationalizations, justifications and vindications so lengthy that the parchment on which it was written trailed to the floor.

Mistress Lackmercy's group consisted of a huge ogre named Brutebogey, brother to the giant who died chasing a mortal boy down a beanstalk, and Madame Screechmore, sister to the witch who was pushed into an oven by a little girl. These three passed the time titillating one another with accounts of cruelties they had imposed, mimicking with particular relish their victims' agonized faces.

In Master Grasp-All's deputation were Rumpelstiltskin and the evil fairy godmother, Madame Pox-Take-You, whose original complaint had led to the congress in the first place. She and Master Grasp-All impeded the group's work with ceaseless fretting, he over being excluded from chairing the Red side, and she for being refused a place on the dais.

On the other side of the magic curtain, Goody Treatwell, Mother Cuddle Up, and the small group of water sprites who had put themselves in charge of the stolen baby spent much of the time sympathizing with their opponents. They could not help likening the curl of Mistress Lackmercy's lip to the snarl of an ill-treated dog and Master Grasp-All's bluster to that of a bully child trying to compensate for the smallness he feels inside. Master Tit-Tat's contentiousness they attributed to the unfortunate face he revealed behind his visor: pocked skin, yellowed teeth, and a distinct cast to the eye. They pictured him as a boy, mercilessly teased at school.

Master Loosepurse's committee comprised the benign sorcerer who had traded powerful magic beans for an ordinary cow, and the contingent of brownies, who brought their cobbling work with them from the gallery. These spent their hour providing everyone (including those on the other side of the curtain) with bread, fruit, and drink aplenty to carry them through the day's deliberations.

Their efforts made the work of Mistress Makepeace's excellent deputation of two considerably easier. Mistress Makepeace was joined by Granny Nimblenoggin, who had cleverly brought Thumbelina into the world as a way to circumvent a curse of barrenness. These clear-seeing, broad-minded sorcerers were not fettered in their thinking by any instinct to defend themselves or their positions. Both had listened carefully in order to understand and evaluate the Red side's arguments, and so could toss back and forth between them, as they pleased, all ideas without restraint.

꒰ꣳ꒱

At last the magic curtain swept back again and the second session began. By unanimous consent of the Blue Chamber, Mistress Makepeace again presided on that side, while Master Grasp-All, having stolen Master Tit-Tat's list when his visor had momentarily swung shut, hurried back to the dais ahead of everyone else and managed to appropriate the presiding seat on the Red side. With diamonds and emeralds dripping from his sleeves and winking in the chandeliers' light, Master Grasp-All held up the long list of arguments enumerated by Master Tit-Tat's committee and opened his mouth to speak, but Mistress Makepeace forestalled him.

"The amendment of spells is known from ancient times," said she. "Recall how the gold imprisoning King Midas's beloved daughter was allowed to melt away the moment the King renounced his greed." A mass of shaking heads demonstrated the Red side's wonder at Mistress Makepeace's ignorance.

Master Tit-Tat threw back his visor with a grating squeak of metal. "The spell should have been let stand and others allowed to benefit from its lesson!" he said.

"But Midas's daughter!" protested Goody Treatwell. "What did the innocent child do to deserve it?" Master Tit-Tat rolled his eyes.

"In a war, my naive Sister, unintended harm is unavoidable."

"But . . But . . " stammered Goody Treatwell.

Mistress Makepeace intervened. "Pray speak to us about this war. What war do you invoke?"

"The war against mortals' arrogance, of course," interrupted Master Grasp-All, attempting to re-establish his ascendancy. "Their trying to usurp power not belonging to them. Your Midas was greedy even for a king."

Mistress Lackmercy bared her gleaming, pointed teeth in a leer and with a sinuous movement of her arms leaned toward Goody Treatwell, who backed away. The evil sorcerer's lizard eyelids lowered lazily as if in contemplation of a slow-moving beetle. "Who says Midas's daughter was innocent?" she said. "Tarnishing among petrified flora in an abandoned palace garden would have been better than the pampered brat deserved." Goody Treatwell blanched at this vision and gratefully accepted Master Loosepurse's offer of reviving salts, which he produced from one of his many pockets.

"Speaking of innocents!" Madame Screechmore, in the back of the hall, curled her bloated fingers around the handle of her broom and pounded the floor for attention. All turned to look. "Think of my fallen sister, who was pushed into her own oven and burned alive by a child." Some of her comrades on the Red side nodded in approval. They could not but admire the slyness of the little girl, even as they deplored the outcome of her actions. " 'Tis the moment to be silent in honor of her memory."

The memorial pause was discomfiting to the Blue side, who considered it unsuitable to honor a malefactor who ate children, yet who could not bear to be unsympathetic to any creature who had lost a relative to a hideous death. The interval (by no means silent, as the goblins made repugnant noises throughout) seemed to go on interminably until Madame Screechmore finally ended it with this declaration: "My colleague has mentioned that we are at war against mortal arrogance and must seek justice—"

"Vengeance!" corrected Master Tit-Tat.

"Indeed. But do we not also cast spells for other reasons? To promote our natural interests, for example, and to survive? Take the case of my poor sister, who conjured a house of sweets to tempt children. Why? Because she must eat, as we all must! Not only the dull venison and berries provided by the forest with seasonal tedium, but once in a while a delicacy. Who does not indulge in a small luxury now and then? Is life worth living without it? People speak as if my sister ate a child every day, but in the matter of children she was known to be virtually abstemious."

"Voracious, you mean!" shouted one of her colleagues. Snorts of derision exploded on her own side of the hall. Madame Screechmore disdained to acknowledge the outburst. "And I blame *wood sprites*," she said, scowling toward the Blue gallery, "for interfering and saving the two children—"

"*Wood sprites, ha!*" grunted the giant, Brutebogey, who sat next to her. "It was the brats themselves who tricked her. Your sister was notoriously slow-witted—"

"Short-*sighted*, not slow-witted! How dare you malign my blood relation!" She struck at him with her broom handle, but he wrenched it from her hand and crushed it to sawdust, quite subduing any impulse she might have had for further protest.

Mistress Makepeace diverted the discussion down more theoretical paths. "There is some truth, perhaps," she said, "in the idea that human beings cannot help being born with some weaknesses. Why not, then, nurture their better selves rather than punish their baser instincts? For example," she turned to the necromancer, "would your prince have thoughtlessly killed your treasured boar if we had worked to foster more consideration for others in our monarchs?"

"What nonsense you speak! They have no better selves. What you call 'consideration for others' is nothing more than self interest, call it what you will, and there is no philanthropist but looks for something in return, if only glory and praise," said Master Tit-Tat.

"We do not seek either glory *or* praise," asserted Master Loosepurse, bristling a little. He had been on the verge of waving a cooling fan at Master Tit-Tat's perspiring face, but with a sudden change of heart drew the fan back and put it in his pocket.

Observing this, Master Tit-Tat sneered, "Do you *not*!" And looked quite pleased to have goaded his opponent into a petty act. Instantly Master Loosepurse rued his unkindness and brought forth the fan again, but Tit-Tat pulled his visor shut. "Too late!" he said hollowly from inside his helmet, "I do not accept favors from hypocrites."

"It is *childish* to call names," snapped Mistress Makepeace, coming to her colleague's defense and therefore raising her voice more than she intended to.

"'Childish,' is that the name you call me?" Master Tit-Tat echoed back.

Embarrassed by her lapse and temporarily at a loss, Mistress Makepeace straightened her starched ruff, which was by no means crooked.

Goody Treatwell hastened to divert the unwelcome attention from her friend. "If the wicked prevail," she said, gesturing toward the audience on the Red side of the floor, "the innocent and powerless will constantly be at a disadvantage. Haven't they trials enough without calamitous spells being cast upon them? Look at the mischief wreaked on the Emperor by scoundrels who convinced the naked man that he was clothed. And this without any magic at all."

"And wasn't the tyrant better for it?" said Master Grasp-All, leaning his chin on his hand with affected boredom.

"Yes, but...that is...I mean that your excesses are unnecessary for chastening humans. They are capable of doing it for each other."

"To the contrary, just at the moment that we are ready to impose a heavy penalty on the wretches, they manage to worm their way out of it, apart from the reprieve you would bestow on them—"

"For instance!" broke in Rumpelstiltskin from the floor. "Until two months ago, I owned a well-trained boy—the grandson of an arrogant queen who married above her station and had to pay the price. But..." the little gnome lamented, "...the ungrateful whelp would not be reconciled to his new surroundings, though I had tethered him to a perfectly good willow sapling that gave middling protection from rain and sun—better than I had in my youth—and the boy eventually caused so much annoyance that he had to be sold to a goblin, who gave little enough for him." Rumpelstiltskin ignored rude chortling from the gallery and rambled for some minutes about this misfortune until sweet-tempered Goody Treatwell blurted out, "Do stop!" and promptly flushed to the ears at her own sharpness.

"Ah," said Mistress Lackmercy, "there it is, you see, that better self you always speak of."

Goody Treatwell said, "I do beg your pardon." Too rattled to speak more, she beseeched Mistress Lackmercy with her eyes, but the sorcerer only laughed.

"You dream foolishly of what can never be," she told the blushing fairy godmother. "It is natural to revert to selfishness. And there is no better teacher than the harsh lessons of retribution."

"Yet I remember the adage of old," spoke up Mistress Makepeace. "'One succeeds better with honey than with vinegar.'"

"Or the adage, older still: 'To spare the rod is to spoil the child.'"

And so they wrangled back and forth, the Blue side's forbearance tried to the utmost and sometimes giving way to an acrimony that went against their nature and racked them afterward with guilt. Idealism was all on the side of the Blue Chamber, but the Red Chamber had the advantage of being willing to use intimidation, lies, rationalizations, and threats in its arguments. After an exhausting session, the two sides separated once again to consult amongst themselves.

In the Red Chamber the meetings were marked by hilarity and self-congratulation. Little work was attempted there, or thought necessary, after the brilliance of the Red side's preceding arguments. In the Blue Chamber the meetings now took on an earnest and somber character.

Master Loosepurse addressed his colleagues. "Could we not leave the issue as it stands," he said, "with the law already in our favor?"

"If we do," Mistress Makepeace replied, "I fear that the malefactors will increase their punishment of mortals one hundredfold. The evil sorcerers cannot work their magic directly upon *us*, and must exact other vengeance for our victory." Her audience could not but agree. "I am afraid the overriding vice of our malfeasant colleagues is that of heartlessness. It is the common trait underlying their greed, vengefulness and cruelty," said Mistress Makepeace, sadly.

"Oh, Sister, it is difficult to imagine a body lacking any sympathy at all!" said Goody Treatwell. Her deep sigh aroused the sleeping tabby in her lap, who yawned, stretched to the tips of its toes, then turned once and curled up again.

"Indeed it is hard to admit that evil cannot be persuaded to be otherwise than evil, but such is the case sometimes. Perhaps we should take a different, more indirect course than simply appealing to their better selves, for I am afraid they have none."

"But you do not suggest we employ deviousness, do you, dear Sister?" asked Goody Treatwell, anxiously.

Mistress Makepeace studied her hands for a moment before answering. "Well, well," she said, "perhaps not exactly."

Master Loosepurse, even as low spirited as he was, did not neglect to hand round another cheering repast to the weary and hungry delegates, including those on the other side of the curtain. While he so provisioned the hall, there was considerable discussion in the Blue Chamber as to the dismal outcomes that would follow upon the triumph of the Red. Mistress Makepeace predicted one eventuality in particular, and on hearing it, Goody Treatwell burst into tears of sympathy. It was at that moment that Mistress Makepeace cast a knowing glance at Granny Nimblenoggin and privately resolved what must be done.

She said, somberly, "Our colleagues on the Red side have shown us that compassion, generosity, and broad-mindedness are not as unassailable as we had thought." Master Loosepurse and Goody Treatwell hung their heads. "Nor can we ignore the malefactors' appeal for fairness." Her gray eyes held steady on the faces of the anxious throng. She paused for a moment. Then, in a clear tone, her voice rang out. "My friends, we will comply with the demand of the Red Chamber."

Gasps went up. Faces filled with dismay. Fairies' wings drooped like petals in the rain. Sprightliness abandoned the sprites, the baby ceased to be bounced upon its caretaker's knee, and the brownies' hammers ceased tapping. Yet none raised an objection, though the suddenness and one-sidedness of Mistress Makepeace's decision took everyone aback. Her wisdom was legendary. No one thought otherwise than to trust her judgment. And Granny Nimblenoggin, detecting something unspoken in her colleague's demeanor, marked it and was reassured.

↰

"The arguments you have presented are sound. Moreover, we wish to be fair." Mistress Makepeace stood before the combined chambers and formally addressed the Red side of the floor.

"You have shown how your proposal may further the moral well-being of weak mortals, for you have demonstrated, even within this great congress, how those of us whose impulse is for good can revert to baser instincts. We congratulate you. You have won the debate upon even terms, and we are ready to draw up a document to that effect."

With one voice the Red Chamber set up a raucous cheering. The goblins and imps leaped onto the demons below in a frenzy of celebration and poured ale down their throats, almost choking them. On the dais, Master Tit-Tat beat his steel gauntlets upon his breastplate, sounding an accompaniment, like crashing cymbals, to the exultation on the floor. Mistress Makepeace waited for the uproar to subside before finishing her declaration. She smiled kindly down at the twelve red-eyed fairy godmothers in the front row, whose knitting, flawed now with a dozen dropped stitches, lay abandoned in their laps.

At last she raised her voice again to the congress. "Upon the signing of this decree by us six chosen representatives," she announced, "we benevolent sorcerers will cease forevermore to interfere with any spell, no matter how pernicious, cast by our malevolent colleagues." Then she stood back from the table to make room for wax, ink, quill and parchment to be placed upon it. The decree was quickly written out, and the six sorcerers stood by to put their seals and signatures to it.

Goody Treatwell was the first to sign. Hugging her purring tabby in the crook of her arm as if for consolation, she bent over the parchment to read the words once through. A tear dropped off the end of her pink nose and smeared a flourish on the legend "Let It Hereby Be Proclaimed..." Sighing mightily, she put her signature and seal to the document and stepped away to make room for Master Loosepurse.

He, too, approached the task with heart so heavy and mind so distressed that he was scarcely able to locate his seal in his deep pocket. The seal, when it was at last found, he duly pressed into the wax, and affixed his signature alongside. Then he deferred to Mistress Makepeace, whose usually composed countenance betrayed a trace of misgiving. Yet she stepped forthrightly to the table and resolutely signed the law.

A momentary silence followed. Even the goblins were struck dumb by the finality of the surrender. Mistress Makepeace then held out the quill for Master Tit-Tat, who was obliged to remove the steel gauntlet on his right hand in order to grasp the slender quill between thumb and forefinger. This procedure resulted in some delay, as his left hand, similarly encumbered, made considerable work in stripping the right hand of its glove, and he would not suffer the indignity of being helped. Mistress Makepeace considerately covered his awkward struggle with a speech.

"I suppose," she said, in a resigned manner, "that hereafter when folk find themselves under wicked spells, and cursed without appeal, the common attitude will be that of grim endurance, as when natural disasters—floods, famines, and wasting illnesses—befall them. Doubtless, they will accept it in the same way, silently, as a thing not to be spoken of. Victims of the inevitable do not like to dwell on evils they cannot escape.

"Folk, I should imagine, will go about their business, plodding along numbly like overworked horses, their imaginations dwindling as they cease to harbor hopes that are sure to be dashed. Curses, and their authors, will not be mentioned. For what would be the use? Then too, it will be feared that complaining could bring on worse." To Master Grasp-All, she addressed herself, musingly: "You spoke with disdain of King Midas's reprieve. I wonder, though, would he or the deity who cursed him be talked about today, a thousand years hence, had the tale ended in utter disaster? Perhaps not. It is understandable. If there is nothing to tell but dismal, final death, where is the story in that?"

Now she uttered a conjectural '*hmm*' and remarked, "It makes one wonder, does it not, whether, if no one had ever heard tell of Midas's story, its participants could truly be said to have existed?" Master Tit-Tat's gauntlet was still only half removed, for he kept pushing back his visor, the better to hear what Mistress Makepeace was saying.

She carried on, still musingly. "The names of benefactors, too, I suppose, will be erased, by this new Order, just as the beauty of a sunrise is seldom noticed where dawn brings another day of suffering. Anonymity does not disturb *us*, of course, for we give comfort, relief and healing for its own sake, not for any fame it may bring us. But I do fear that the world under these new conditions may be somewhat bleak for *your* kind, and for that, I am truly sorry. 'Tis perhaps colorless enough to be without a heart, but how much more desolate to live without the recognition from others that you so enjoy." Master Tit-Tat paused in his struggle with the gauntlet. Master Grasp-All frowned. Mistress Lackmercy arched an eyebrow suspiciously.

Cocking her head a little and gazing at the now empty Red gallery, Mistress Makepeace continued absently, almost as if she were talking to herself, "Before today, when evil curses and spells were amenable to revision, folks cogitated over and discussed the wicked enchantments that befell them. They ran to their neighbors to confer and gossip and recount their own tales and those of others. The malefactors who cursed them were notorious, their exploits told with a certain relish at hearths and in nurseries. Children thrilled one another with the exploits of goblins, demons and ogres, for bad fortune is more interesting with the possibility of a reversal.

"I contemplate a dull, dank world now, of incessant, unrelenting woe where the names of malefactors are erased from mortal minds and no longer fabled or even spoken of." She turned earnestly toward the Red Chamber. "Please believe that it was never our intention to call such obscurity down upon you," she said. "I feel great compassion for the change in status you will henceforth undergo."

Master Tit-Tat had extricated his right hand, which was held out to receive the quill Mistress Makepeace still proffered. But his hand remained uncertainly in the air as he peered through the slit of his visor, his eyes darting back and forth from one to the other of his allies. Master Grasp-All and Mistress Lackmercy, too, seemed poised in attitudes of consternation. Grasp-All's fingers gripped his beard and Lackmercy's lip curled in a severe arch to match the one in her brow. None of the three moved, but stood staring at Mistress Makepeace.

Master Tit-Tat thought, *"Artless fool! Incapable of putting a stopper in her bleeding heart,"* and warned himself, *"Say nothing to reveal that her nobility will save us from our own undoing!"*

Master Grasp-All studied the faces of Mistress Makepeace and those of her two allies for some evidence of guile in their expressions. His belly was still full of the bread, plums, and mead that Master Loosepurse had sent over during the last deliberations. *"These gulls are capable of the most naive, self-defeating generosity,"* he concluded.

Mistress Lackmercy stared hard at her benevolent opponent. She did not doubt for a moment that Mistress Makepeace's sympathy was a pretense, for compassion itself was a pretense.

"A word only, used to define a nonexistent emotion," thought she. Yet she could not deny the three signatures on the document or the sadness of its signers. Nor could she ignore the truth in Mistress Makepeace's speculations, and this, above all, turned her spine icy with fear, for the thought of her own obscurity was the one thing she could not face.

Suddenly she snatched the quill from Mistress Makepeace's hand and viciously snapped it in two. "We do not consent to sign," she said, and hearing this, Master Grasp-All and Master Tit-Tat between them seized the parchment and tore it asunder.

With that, the agreement was rendered null and void and the great congress dissolved.

ى

Thus, we still can say that each cloud has a silver lining, and it is always darkest before the dawn, and we find the old tales as interesting now as they were in ancient days. And there continues to be bad in us and good in us, which cannot but struggle, ever and anon, within the deepest places in our hearts. Sometimes the struggle sounds like the pounding of a steel glove on a hollow breastplate. Other times it is like the busy tapping of a dozen little hammers.